She'd saved his life...

Rafe Hawk refused to accept the inheritance, of a large English estate, and the title that goes with it, after his birth father's death because the man chose duty over the woman he loved and their son.

When he finds himself temporarily living at Kinsale Hall, he's not prepared to trust anyone associated with the place, including Trudi Delaney and her daughter.

So why, when he looks into their eyes, does he suddenly remember a woman who vanished without a trace after saving his life one stormy night eleven years earlier?

Now he could destroy hers.

Something more than the handsome American's instant dislike of her, disturbs Trudi Delaney. Why, when he'd come to design some chalets for her, does he spend so much of his time in areas of Kinsale Hall off-limits to visitors?

Trudi—who is still plagued with nightmares of her entrapment in a brutal five year marriage where she was held a prisoner of her cruel and psychotic husband—has been a single parent for more a decade.

Eleven years after the night she and an unidentified man barely escaped with their lives, Trudi is still unable to remember the hours she spent with this stranger—the hours in which her beautiful daughter was conceived. Now, more than a decade later, she is confronted by another stranger. Will this one destroy everything she holds dear?

She knew better than to trust him. At least she thought she did.

"What are you doing here?"

"We have to talk."

"I've nothing to say to you. Go away. I want to be alone."

"Where are you going?" Cautiously, Rafe moved forward.

Did he assume that like the fawn, now vanished, she too might bolt away?

"It's none of your business." Emotionally drained and feeling too tired to talk, Trudi put her hand out to repel his advance. Why couldn't he leave her alone? "Go away," she repeated, without any real hope he'd listen.

With a sigh, she watched him approach and, as if in a dream, stared as his hand wrapped gently around the top of her arm before he guided her to a nearby fallen tree trunk.

"You have nothing to fear from me." He sat at the other end of the trunk, putting some distance between them.

"You don't know anything about it. Stay out of my affairs and go away."

"That's not possible. If Rachel is my daughter, do you expect me to turn my back on the result of the most wonderful night of lovemaking I've ever experienced? She's a grand kid, and I'd want her to know I'm her Dad."

"Lust, Rafe. Nothing more than lust. Admit it."

"How can you be sure? Vince said you don't remember what happened."

"Oh, Vince told you, did he?" she spat at him. "How convenient!"

Trudi watched the dull red stain sweep up Rafe's neck and into his face. How could he expect her to share Rachel when he held her in contempt? It couldn't work.

KUDOS FOR DUTY CALLS

You have a knack for showing beautiful, almost poetic descriptions and depth of emotions. Your talent for describing natural settings and descriptions takes my breath away. You depict the sexual sparks between Trudi and Rafe well using detail that humanizes your characters and makes them a good match for long term love. -- *Judy, crit group member*

You have a unique and exceptional writing style and voice. Your physical descriptions of the world around your characters are very alive and real to the reader. -- *Valerie, crit group member*

This is good, really good. Usually, I don't like a lot of narrative, but I found myself totally enjoying it. You do a wonderful job of arousing the reader"s interest by creating the mystery surrounding the hero. Also the way you reveal things keeps the reader interested and moves the plot forward. I like your characters. This is absolutely wonderful. -- *Sandra, crit group member*

The dialogue is skilfully handled and shows the different characters perfectly. -- *Rebecca, crit group member*

Great story. I envy your capacity for drawing the setting so well, it has great descriptions. -- *Sabrina, crit group member*

A beautiful tale, told by a master storyteller. Gloag has managed to take the delicate issue of abused women and handle it with sensitivity and compassion. -- *Pepper, published author*

DUTY CALLS

By

SHERRY GLOAG

A BLACK OPAL BOOKS PUBLICATION

Genre: Contemporary Romance

DUTY CALLS
Copyright © 2011 by Sherry Gloag All Rights Reserved
PRINT ISBN: 978-1-937329-01-3

Cover Art by Pepper O'Neal
Copyright © 2011 All Rights Reserved

Published by Black Opal Books http://www.blackopalbooks.com

DEDICATION

Duty Calls is dedicated to Ian with thanks
for all his love, support, and encouragement.

And to Dean for his enthusiasm.

CHAPTER 1

Exasperated, Rafe Hawk shifted his gaze from the window to his mother, a petite woman, sitting serenely on the sofa in front of him.

"We've covered this ground before. What more do I have to say, before you acknowledge I want nothing to do with Daniel's estates?" Rafe's glance flicked over the open letter lying on the table between them. "He may have sired me, but that doesn't make him my father."

Funnelling his fingers through his hair, he continued. "How many times do I have to say no? No, I will not go back." He stuffed his fists into his pockets in an effort to conceal his rising frustration from Martha Hawk. "I don't give a damn whether Kinsale Hall is entailed to me or the man in the moon. Why should I?

"Only Daniel Kinsale and his solicitors knew I'd arranged to meet him. I told no one I'd changed my schedule and arrived in England a week earlier than expected, and yet Denny Cadmore somehow discovered both my plans and identity."

Rafe glared at his parent. "Given those facts, tell me why I should stake a claim on a god-forsaken English estate, when everything and everyone who means anything to me lives here in The States?"

The drone of the old-fashioned overhead fan broke the ensuing silence. The oppressive heat stalked through the room sapping the energy from anyone or anything in its path.

"Rafe you're making me dizzy. Sit down and stop prowling around the room." His mother patted the cushions beside her. "How many times do I have to tell you, you were born from love, not lust? Whether you like it or not, you are the legitimate heir to your father's estate."

A shaft of sunlight caught a few silvery streaks in her blonde hair.

"But born out of wedlock," Rafe snapped, before realizing the words had queued up for release.

"Yes, out of wedlock." She sighed. "I've never denied it, nor have I stolen your entitlement to your birth name. Your birth father—" She paused for a few seconds.

"Daniel loved me," she continued on a wistful note. "I accepted he couldn't divorce his wife and agreed we had no future together, only the present. I've explained why he felt duty bound to uphold his family's expectations. Having you gave me reason to survive without Daniel. You are from the man of my heart."

Rafe's free hand crashed down on the table, sending the letter floating to the floor. "If he loved you so much, how come another of his bastards crawled out of the woodwork? One whose birth certificate proves he's ten days younger than me? How come the same bastard damn near sent me to my grave? Explain that if you can."

Smoke-gray eyes glared into violet ones until with another thump of his fist, Rafe rose from the settee and stalked back to the window to gaze unseeingly at the cheerful riot of colors in his mother's flowerbeds.

"For God's sake, Mother, Kinsale two-timed you whilst declaring his undying love for you, and you fell for it!"

Unsolicited, a vision of the man rose in his memory. Similar in height, Daniel's thatch of silver hair replaced the honey-blonde tresses Rafe saw in the mirror every time he shaved.

The same familiar smoky gray eyes, full of hope and yet displaying a lifetime's regret, had stared back at Rafe in the smoke-filled library over a decade ago. He remembered the timbre of his birth-father's deep voice, while he explained the intricacies of English property laws and entailment. Because of recent changes in the legislation, an incumbent of entailed property could leave it to someone of his own choice.

The sense of dislocation still haunted Rafe.

He recalled the deep, rich-plum leather wing chairs, the wood fire blazing in the hearth, and Lord Kinsale demanding Rafe uphold his duty to the estate and accept the responsibilities he would inherit when Daniel died. Those same responsibilities had separated Daniel and Rafe's mother all his life.

Rafe owed nothing to his birthfather or the estate. Nothing at all!

Not then. Not now. His only duty included his mother, siblings, Jess, his stepfather, and Rafe's clients. And that's the way he liked it.

Didn't he?

So, why did the memory of an unknown woman with amber-colored eyes still haunt him?

"Daniel suffered a breakdown after his father died." His mother's voice interrupted Rafe's thoughts. "He rang me the day after his father's funeral. He admits he went out and drank himself into oblivion and woke up the next morning in an unfamiliar room with a woman he'd never seen before. The woman claimed they'd gone back to her place for sex. Three months later she turned up at the Hall claiming he'd got her pregnant. It's the oldest scam in the world, for God's sake.

"They didn't have DNA testing in those days which meant he had no way of proving otherwise. I believed him. She even named Daniel as the father on the child's birth certificate." His mother's plea for understanding slipped right over Rafe's head.

"Rafe, love at first sight does happen. Believe me, my life changed the moment I set eyes on Daniel. Love at first sight is not easy to explain," she said with a wistful sigh.

"I won't go back," Rafe insisted, his back to the room. He refused to let the sound of his mother's soft voice influence his decision. "Daniel put duty to his English family and his estate workers before the woman he proclaimed to love and the son she bore him. How can you blame me if I put my own family first?"

He'd grown up hating his birth father for walking away from them then and now hated the ghost whose influence still reached beyond the grave.

From a small boy's point of view, his birth father's involvement with his English estates meant he'd taken the easy way out by compensating for his absence in Rafe's life with money.

Rafe had become one more responsibility dictated by duty to be honored. Why else would Daniel refuse to meet his son until he'd stared mortality in the face eleven years ago? Rafe didn't need or want Daniel's estates, and he certainly hadn't expected them to almost cost him his life.

"It makes no sense," his mother admonished. "Jess may be your stepfather but there are thousands of kids who never experience the unconditional love he gives you. You insult Jess with your ingratitude." She pinned him with a cold stare. "Some might call you a hypocrite."

"Really?" Unbridled fury spun Rafe round to glare down at his mother. "What about you? You claim Daniel was the love of your life, but you married Jess while loving someone else. So what right do you have to criticize me? Smells strongly of hypocrisy to me."

He swung away, inhaled slowly in an effort to control his rising temper, then spun back again. "And how does Jess feel, knowing your heart will always belong to someone else? Someone who put us at the bottom of his list of priorities? And you accuse me of insulting Jess? I'm not the hypocrite here.

"Jeez, I could end up like Jess and find myself married to a woman who loves another man." He raked his fingers through his hair. "With examples like those, can you blame me for lacking the inclination for marriage and children?"

"If that's your attitude it's a good thing you don't intend to have any children."

Behind his mother's shrug, he saw the hurt in her eyes. Rarely did she strike back, verbally or otherwise, and guilt quashed Rafe's spurt of anger.

"I'm sorry. That was out of line."

"Yes, Rafe, it was. And I expect you to apologise to you mother," Jess snapped from the doorway. "The reason your mother and I married is not your concern. I'll never love another woman. Your mother is the center of my universe. And I'm the lucky man who holds her in my arms every night and wakes up beside her every morning.

"It grieves me to discover you still hold such resentment against Daniel. And it saddens me that you use him as an excuse for not trusting in life and in love enough to embrace it and create the chance of having a family of your own." Jess crossed the room and dropped down beside his wife, resting his arm along the back of the settee before addressing Rafe again. "I hope you don't wake up one day and discover the world left you behind because you were too busy enjoying your own private pity-party."

Rafe couldn't remember the last time Jess's words cut so deep. *Pity-party!* He enjoyed women, rewarded them handsomely when they went their separate ways. He valued his independence and the knowledge no-one else controlled his emotions. And yet Jess directed a glance at him that still reduced him to an errant ten-year-old.

"What about your friend Arthur? Do you intend to renege on your agreement to design those retirement apartments he's commissioned?" Martha Hawk's softly spoken query snapped Rafe's attention back to the present.

"No, I won't, but I may shelve it for six months until I've finished designing Dr. Swanlow's medical center.

"You're making excuses."

The frustration riding on his shoulders slipped away. "What if I am?" Rafe shot his mother the audacious grin that had saved him from many childhood reprimands. "That gives you another six months to be a pain in my—"

"Rafe! Don't you dare say it. Would I do such a thing?"

"As if you wouldn't, more like." Treading swiftly across the room he bent down to engulf his mother in a bear hug.

෴

"Stop the car!" Rafe swung round to face the driver. "I recognize this road. You never told me the commission to build those retirement units involved Kinsale Hall. You knew damn well I swore eleven years ago never set foot in the place again."

Rage hazed his vision. "And because you withheld that vital information, Arthur, consider this contract null and void."

Rafe shot forward in his seat when his friend from their Uni days tramped on the brakes.

Arthur Clifton skewed round in his seat. "How long have we known each other?"

Startled by the question, Rafe hesitated. "What's the length of our friendship got to do with anything? Other than the fact you're stretching it paper thin if you believe I'll set foot on Kinsale territory again."

He swung open the car door and leaped out, his fingers tunnelling through his windswept hair. Brilliant blue skies overhead offered a large playground for the early summer sunshine and the fluffy white clouds sailing by. He spotted the high chimney tops through the trees.

"Do you really imagine I'd bring you here without a specific reason?" Arthur remained in his seat, his hands on the steering wheel, watching Rafe pace up and down the soft verge beside the open-topped car.

"I can't think of a single reason good enough to justify resurrecting memories I'd rather forget. That misadventure nearly cost me my life and possibly the life of an unknown woman." His fist slammed onto the gleaming car bonnet, silencing the nearby birdsong. "Take me back to Heathrow." He yanked at his soft, blue-silk shirt collar and loosened his tie. "I agreed to this commission as a favor. I'm up to my eyeballs in contracts right now and don't need this one at the best of times, and now…" Once again Rafe's hand shot through his hair.

"Please?" Arthur's gaze held his. Dark, intense, and something else Rafe couldn't identify.

"No."

He leaned into the car, hooked his jacket off the apology for a back shelf and dug out his cell phone. "Fine. I'll call for a taxi."

"You won't get one to come out this far in a hurry."

Arthur's certainty fuelled Rafe's anger. He stalked round the car to the trunk and yanked it open. Thankfully, he'd only brought a carry-on bag with enough to tide him over a short two-day stay in the UK. He'd hitch a ride if forced to.

Arthur's hand clamped down on his arm before he lifted the bag free. "Hear me out."

When Rafe nodded agreement, he released Rafe's arm and stepped back. Arthur slammed the trunk shut and leaned against it. He waited until Rafe settled his butt against the vehicle beside him before he spoke.

"You don't need me to remind you about Denny Cadmore, I'm sure."

A vision of the heavy-set, swarthy-faced man who'd set him up swam in front of Rafe. Eleven years hadn't diminished the details—black hair, a neck resembling the trunk of an ancient oak tree, and coal-black eyes, mean and red-rimmed by the end of the evening's cards. He'd lacked a couple inches of Rafe's six-feet, but his shoulders and chest equalled those of an enormous English carthorse. And Cadmore's cohorts—

Rafe had been lucky to escape their machinations that night. He owed his life to an unknown woman who led him to safety through the wildest storm he'd ever experienced.

"No, I don't need any reminders of my last visit regarding the Kinsale Estate," he confirmed.

"I never discovered how you managed to evade the executors of the will after Lord Kinsale's death," Arthur lied. "But when they couldn't trace you, they got in touch with Cadmore. Apparently, he managed to convince them of the legitimacy of his claim, and he moved from London to live at the Hall for the next five years."

"Five years? Why only five years?" Curiosity, Rafe convinced himself.

"He died in a turf-war shooting."

Arthur's sudden air of innocence didn't fool Rafe. Arthur and his boss, Vince Parker, carried the responsibility for England's national security. So getting rid of a scumbag like Cadmore would have been child's play.

"I suppose you invoked some national security code, somehow."

"I do believe the papers mentioned something about drug overlords." Arthur shifted from studying the countryside to staring at Rafe. "I doubt you heard. The executors traced his widow, who now lives at the Hall."

"Widow? Cadmore never said anything about a wife. He introduced me to his sister. I told you he wagered his sister against my twenty thousand pounds."

The remembered stench of the dingy room, stale beer, and dirty, sweaty bodies that fateful night pervaded Rafe's memory. The single overhead bulb that failed to illuminate the far corners of the room hid the gray-faced stick of a woman who'd stepped forward when commanded. The memory of her straggly, dirty, shoulder length hair, wide frightened eyes and hands that sought refuge in the skimpy black cotton skirt hanging limply against her bare legs, still haunted his dreams. And turned them into nightmares.

Rafe swallowed. No way could he kid himself. The memories of that night would haunt him for the rest of his life. He'd treated her like a side of beef hanging in a butcher's shop in an effort to maintain a cover already blown.

The storm.

Their flight from the house.

The river.

And when they'd been pulled from the raging torrents, she'd adamantly refused to let the medics take her to hospital. Images he'd rather forget flashed through his mind. The comfort they sought in each other's arms and the realization life might have ceased for both of them that night. Comfort changed to awareness and awareness to a commemoration of life in their coming together. It transcended logic or lust. It became a need to celebrate their survival. Her disappearance the following morning ran through his mind like an old movie.

"I have a copy of the marriage license."

Arthur's words didn't make sense, but on the other hand they did. A macabre kind of sense that sent shivers down his spine.

"So they traced the widow and installed her at Kinsale Hall," Rafe said. "I fail to understand why you should consider it 'special' enough to haul me across the Atlantic to spend time designing units for a place I vowed never to set foot in again."

If it took anger to banish the decade-old memories Rafe would use it, regardless of whether his long-time, school friend deserved it or not.

Arthur shifted against the car to hold Rafe's gaze before speaking. "I don't have to remind you of Vince, do I?"

"Of course not. But what's he got to do with this?"

"After Cadmore's death, and before they discovered the existence of his widow, Vince and I contacted the executors and asked them to allow us the use of the Hall as a Safe House and retirement center for our agents. When everything was up and running, we asked them to install Cadmore's widow in the role of general overseer for our people and the estate."

"And?"

"They agreed."

"I still don't understand why you've called me in on this." Rafe pushed away from his perch against the car trunk, paced off and back again. He threw his jacket back into the car and glared at his companion.

"We have to select people we can trust to work on projects at the Hall for security reasons," Arthur said. "We don't need an architect planning units for the place who may pass the designs to nefarious parties to use at a later date. You've been cleared."

"Bull." Rafe's snort frightened a skylark from its nearby nest and sent the bird soaring into the sky, chattering all the way up until it became a small black dot against the overhead canopy of blue. "You must have hundreds of in-house staff and outsiders on retainer who pass your security."

"I don't deny it." Arthur's ready agreement startled Rafe into stillness. "But none of them are aware of the existence of the Hall. And we want things to remain that way."

The beat of silence stretched from one minute to five. Rafe searched Arthur's face for a trace of deception and found none. Nevertheless, he couldn't quite quash his conviction Arthur's request included a hidden agenda.

Could he do it? Could Rafe enter the building that epitomised everything he hated about his origins? All the actions and reactions that had him standing at the side of the road with his friend, facing...

What?

If he kept his past where it belonged, he could scope out the site for these retirement units, then head back home to Boston and draw up the plans. He didn't need to stay on-site to maintain contact with the local authorities for planning information.

"Twenty-four hours," he snapped and flung himself back into the passenger seat.

ↄ◡ↄ◡ↄ

"I'd like to sit outside."

Bella's frail voice reached Trudi Delaney from the small room they called the 'snug.' She closed her account book and shifted the file into her top drawer before locking it.

"It's lovely outside." She knelt beside Bella and helped her to her feet. "We can have our meal out on the patio if it's warm enough for you. The girls would love to 'picnic' after a hard day in school." Her gurgle of laughter filled the air.

Both their daughters enjoyed school, but they enjoyed coming home more.

The girls, born minutes apart, were closer than some twins, although unrelated.

After seeing her friend settled, Trudi pulled up another chair and leaned back to let the sun warm her upturned face. Birdsong filled the comfortable silence between the two women.

"I want to talk to you about Blackwater Farm," Bella said, after a few moments.

"How come you happen to own the farm next door to Kinsale Hall," Trudi asked. "And why have you never lived there?" She studied Bella's face.

Bella's third and final battle with cancer may have robbed her of her beauty, but it failed to diminish her spirit. And Trudi knew she rarely complained.

"My uncle left the farm to me a few weeks before Lizzie's birth," Bella began. "He claimed to have more money than sense and had no use for the place. He expected me to take more care of it." Her sigh landed in the silence between them. "Somehow he discovered my marriage was in trouble. I feel so guilty for letting the farm go to wrack and ruin."

"You have nothing to feel guilty about. But why didn't you move in after your husband abandoned you?"

"Because I suspected he knew about the place."

"But you agreed to move in here with me. I mean, the farm's only half a mile away if you take the path through the woods."

"True, but when I talked to Vince and your brother about it and about Lizzie's safety, they promised me the residents would care for us. They assured me they'd be happier if we lived at the Hall and tried to imply we'd be doing them a huge favor if I agreed. You know what those two are like. I can't decide which brother is the most devious, yours or mine."

Trudi swore under her breath when pain strangled Bella's laugh before it fully formed.

"But that's not what I wanted to talk about," Bella said after regaining her breath.

"Okay. I'm listening."

"The last time Vince visited, we discussed the implications of leaving the farm to Lizzie outright, as opposed to leaving it to you, in trust for Lizzie later."

"*What?*" Trudi shot to her feet. "Why would you do that? Thanks to our brothers, I'm firmly entrenched here with the legal pink ribbons to guarantee I—and therefore *we*—stay here."

"What will you do when you regain the missing hours of your memory?" Bella demanded.

"Nothing. You and I both know the doctors maintain the longer the memory loss continues the less likely I will ever regain it."

"But you're not happy here, are you?"

"I should be." Trudi admitted. But somehow, for some inexplicable reason, she never considered she belonged in these sumptuous surroundings. Perhaps her late husband's prior occupancy of the Hall tainted her ability to settle. "The girls love it," she added, more forcefully than she intended.

"But I notice you're keeping them close to the house. Why?" Anxiety lurked in Bella's eyes.

Damn. Trudi hid her fists behind her back. If Bella noticed her caution with the girls, had anyone else? The number of permanent residents fell from ten to three a month ago—Judy Strathallan, a relative newcomer, and the Frobishers, who'd lived here for three years now. All three had formerly worked in the field for the security of the country. Trudi assumed little got passed them. Had they noticed the intruder? And how to answer Bella's query without adding to her concern?

"Mr. Peach from the village hardware store mentioned someone was asking questions around," Trudi said. "So as a precaution I asked the girls to stay close."

"Did they find out what they wanted?" Bella asked, a frown pleating her forehead.

"I haven't been into the village since. No one's mentioned anything. Therefore, I imagine they've moved on."

"But you continue to keep the girl's close?"

"They have exams coming up. It doesn't hurt to have them focus on their schoolwork." Trudi's snort of laughter joined with Bella's.

"You're such a bad liar. I'll take pity on you and shut up. But don't assume you've sidetracked our talk about the farm. I've asked Vince to have the documents drawn up, and he's bringing them down for you to sign, next time he's here. And—" She raised her hand before Trudi interrupted. "Look at it this way, if you accept it, and Lizzie doesn't want it when she comes of age, you will always have somewhere of your own for you and Rachel."

"That's hardly fair to Lizzie."

"She's in agreement. Vince and I discussed it with her during his last visit. When I'm gone, you become her legal mother and are entitled to protect her interests until she's of age."

"She's only ten years old, how can she make such a big decision?"

"Both our girls are wise beyond their years," Bella snapped. "Give me this, Trudi. Let me go with a peaceful mind."

Trudi swallowed her grief and nodded. She'd discuss it with Vince when he next visited.

"Thank you," Bella said with a smile. "I'm expecting him later this afternoon."

"You haven't lost that sneaky streak, have you?"

"Nope." Bella's smile never dimmed as she turned the conversation. "How about a cup of tea and some of the gorgeous lemon cake you made last night?"

When Trudi had served Bella her snack, she headed to her own room to collect a pile of files she'd taken from her office and worked on through the previous night.

The nightmares didn't come so frequently now, but when they did, they banished any further chance of sleep.

Initially, after the dreams, she'd tried forcing her memory to search for something, anything, that might reveal the face of the man who'd fathered her child— something to explain why she'd slept with another man while still married to her bastard of a husband.

Kept a virtual prisoner by the man she'd married, how come she'd escaped, let alone met someone who'd given her the gift of such a wonderful daughter?

She often wondered about the night Rachel was conceived. But whatever happened, she couldn't doubt the treasured outcome.

She looked round at the wood-panelled walls. They advertised the legacy and history of the building, but she hated the darkness saturating the room.

Even if she'd wanted to, the preservation order on the building prevented her from painting over the dark wood. To alleviate the gloom she'd selected light furniture and fittings. Pale cream curtains hung at the window. A light honey-colored cover over the bed complemented the light cherry-wood headboard. Full length mirrors fronted her cupboards and reflected the natural light from the window into the room. Two desks stood sentinel on either side of the window. Open files spread across the surface of one, while her computer and loaded inbox stood on the other.

She crossed the room and gathered up the scattered files. Searching in the drawers for several more, she piled them up in her arms before retracing her steps downstairs.

CHAPTER 2

Head down and deep in thought, it took a moment for Trudi to work out the unexpected shadows across the hall floor before she looked toward the source. Two men, one familiar.

"Arthur." With a delighted shriek, Trudi dropped her armful of files and flew into her brother's outstretched arms. "What are you doing here?" She gave him a smacking kiss on his lips. "I didn't expect to see you for a while, not with the baby due any time now. How is Serena?"

She stepped out of Arthur's arms and looked into his face. "Shouldn't you be at home? Is something wrong?"

"Hey, babe, it's good to see you, too, and so many questions." Arthur beamed at her.

The sight of the tight-lipped stranger standing behind her brother diluted her smile and dispelled her normal welcome.

"How's my best girl Rachel?" Arthur's voice refocused her attention.

"She's good, better than good." Trudi smiled her mother's pride for her daughter.

"Lizzie?" Arthur's question threatened to shatter Trudi's smile. Sweet Lizzie, Rachel's best friend and Bella's daughter. She knew her brother saw the shimmer of tears in her eyes and understood her struggle for control.

"What if I'm not enough?" she whispered.

"Lizzie loves you, hon, and it's what Bella wants."

"I know, but sometimes I'm scared for her." She inhaled a deep breath. Aware Arthur was watching her pull herself together, she straightened her spine. "Thank you for reminding me." Gratefully she leaned into Arthur's fingers as he gently brushed them across her cheek.

꿍꿍꿍

Something shifted within Rafe when he observed the golden-haired beauty walk from the shadows into the full glare of the sunlight streaming through the open front door. He'd studied her for a full minute before she became aware of their presence.

She was tall and slender with curves in all the right places. Rafe imagined the feel of her in his arms. A drift of shoulder length hair fell forward as she studied a file on top of the pile. The faint scent of her perfume wafted toward him, reminding him of roses still wet with a summer morning's dew, drawing him in, fuelling a need in him.

He wanted to alleviate the sorrow he sensed within her, to wrap her in his arms and taste her lips covering his while her body pressed up against him. The strong connection to a woman he'd never seen before consumed him, and he wondered why his soul cried out in recognition.

On second thought, he decided, he didn't want to know anything at all. Her shriek as she launched herself into Arthur's arms shattered his fantasies, reminding him he didn't need this, or any other, woman. With rising contempt, Rafe watched the golden-haired siren wrap her arms around his friend's neck before giving him a smacking kiss on his lips—his married friend, whose wife expected to give birth to their baby any time now.

He noticed how her generous curves fit snugly in Arthur's long and slender hands. Her skimpy, faded-pink tank-top, clinging to the voluptuous curves of her breasts now plastered against his friend's chest, left little to the imagination. The fall of luxuriant shoulder-length hair still concealed her face when she rested her head against Arthur's shoulder. The soft tone of her voice curled Rafe's toes when she responded to his friend's comment.

The unexpected sense of betrayal almost buckled his knees.

Arthur's betrayal cut deep as he returned the siren's kisses while his pregnant wife waited for him at home. The woman wrapped herself around him like a lover even though she knew about the baby's imminent arrival. And the intimate conversation between them revealed a depth and longevity to an apparently devious relationship Rafe never anticipated from Arthur.

If he'd stood his ground and refused the commission, Rafe fumed, he'd have avoided witnessing what looked like a nasty, messy affair between Arthur and the woman who wanted Rafe's designs. Spinning on his heel, he started toward the door to go back to the car and wait for Arthur to take him back to London.

"I'm sorry." The woman's soft husky voice whispered over him, caressing his skin. The sound travelled through him and settled deep within. His feet refused to move.

"You must consider us awfully rude. I'm Trudi Delaney." She extended her hand in his direction while glancing back at Arthur. "Please introduce us."

"Trudi, meet my friend Rafe Hawk. I've commissioned him to design those chalets you're after. He's come to check the site and discuss the project with you."

"Oh! Thank you, Mr Hawk." Her lips parted slightly as she placed her hand in his. "If you can make my dream come true, I'll be eternally grateful to you."

The touch of her fingertips sent a jolt of electricity clear down to his soul. He wanted to pull his hand away. Instead, he presented a façade of calmness to mask his rising anger. Pinning a polite smile on his face, he returned the handshake before shoving his fist into his trouser pocket. How could she churn him up until he didn't know which way was up? This wanton shamelessly carried on an affair with a man whose baby even now waited to make its appearance in the world.

Why waste time imagining the taste of those lips on his? His heart shouldn't stutter at the sight of a woman so lacking in moral integrity. Seeing her arms wrapped around his friend shouldn't parch his throat with desire. Her curvaceous breasts pushed up against Arthur's chest shouldn't have Rafe aching to hold them in the palms of his hands, tease them with his tongue, or suckle them like a lover.

She wore flat shoes he noted, and yet her gaze came level with his. And still he wanted her.

His mother's words drifted through his haze of desire.

'Until it hits you, you can't conceive the power of love.'

Yeah, right! This amounted to nothing more than a raging bout of lust. He had no desire to become this woman's victim in either love or lust. Nor did he want her gratitude for fulfilling her dream.

For the sake of a waning friendship, he'd complete this assignment before flying home to inform his mother the estate, supposedly entailed to him, boasted a current and apparently legal tenant, and therefore didn't need its rightful heir.

℃℈℈

One good look at the newcomer and Trudi's familiar world tilted on its axis. Like two souls meeting at a level beyond words, beyond destiny. The shockwaves travelled right down to her toes. A breath begging for release whooshed out of her lungs, leaving her shaken. She couldn't remember experiencing such feelings before.

Impossible. Nothing had changed, and yet in that second, everything changed. She'd changed.

And she didn't know how or why.

Any man she eyeballed must top six feet. His honey-blond hair kissed his shirt collar and framed his square-set jaw and sun-bronzed skin.

Encased in a light-blue silk shirt, his shoulders were to die for. Gray designer pants sheathed hard-muscled thighs. And his hands, wide and square—and totally unlike the artistic, long-fingered hands she envisioned holding an architect's pen—radiated warmth that crept up her arm. How would they feel if they caressed her body?

The uncompromising, hard line of his sensuous lips startled her out of her reverie. She rocked back on her heels as she recognized his unconcealed contempt. What had she done to warrant such alienation?

He'd come to do a job. Once he completed his designs he'd go home, and she'd never see him again. Why should she care? He meant nothing to her. She didn't want any man's arms holding her prisoner. Certainly not this one's.

She had Rachel and soon Lizzie to think about. She wasn't prepared to jeopardize their futures by giving up her independence.

"I'm not familiar with the procedure, Mr Hawk." Satisfied the quiet steady tone of her voice covered her swirling emotions, she continued. "If I show you the site and explain my ideas, will you require any other information before you and Arthur leave?" Without being downright rude to the man, she could hardly make it plainer she didn't want him or his attitude here.

"Well, before we do anything else Trudi, love, I'd like a cup of coffee. I'm parched." Arthur swung a casual arm across her shoulders and pulled her across the hallway and into a large book-lined study to their left.

Rafe gathered the scattered files from the floor and followed them into the library his father had led him to eleven years ago. Neatly stacked papers covered the old mahogany desk placed in front of open French-doors. He put the files he rescued beside them. An old brass lamp stood sentinel on the corner of the desk, and bright colored plastic trays on the other end of the desktop cast an endearing human touch to the workspace.

On the matching carved mahogany sideboard against the wall, to his left, he spied a large tray holding a coffee machine, kettle, and several brightly colored mugs. Arthur held up an empty mug, one eyebrow raised in silent query.

"Coffee, thanks." Rafe moved to the book shelves and began studying the titles. Had she added any of her own books to the ones occupying the now lemon scented shelves he'd seen over a decade ago? The scent of ancient cigars, enjoyed by former generations, no longer lingered in the room. "You have a nice place here, Ms. Delaney," he said, watching her take the mug Arthur held out to her.

"Thank you." She offered a warm and sincere smile. "It's beautiful, and I am lucky to live here."

"Lucky? What has luck to do with it?"

"I consider myself more in the role of a curator than an owner," she replied.

Rafe tried to identify the emotion in her voice. She sounded almost wistful, but why? He sensed undercurrents running beneath her words.

"Forgive me for asking, but do you have the authority to commission these twelve units, if as you say, you don't own the property? I refuse to become embroiled in some ownership dispute, either now or in the future." He turned to Arthur. "Perhaps it's best if we leave when you've finished your coffee." Rafe placed his empty mug on the sideboard and started toward the open door.

He'd had enough and wanted to go. Ghosts of the past still stalked the room now occupied by a woman whose presence lit the darkest corners of his soul. Corners he never intended to shed light on.

"Don't be silly, Trudi." Arthur said, ignoring Rafe's outburst. "We've hashed this to death before. Under the circumstances, you inherited this place fair and square. And when the time comes Rachel will inherit the Hall from you."

"You inherited this place?" Rafe struggled to keep the contempt out of his voice. "How come you said you are the curator if you inherited the place?"

"It came to me through my husband." She moved to place her mug on the desk.

℅℅℅

Trudi recognized the smile her brother flashed toward Rafe. "What are you up to Arthur?"

Her brother's feigned innocence didn't fool her. After all, they'd wasted too many hours arguing over her concerns about the building of these chalets. Only last week he'd said, "Leave it with me. I know just the man to design your chalets. And he's already cleared by security."

She'd given in. "You're talking about your American friend, I presume?" She hadn't been pleased. "Why can't you call in your usual builder? He's cleared with security and already under contract."

"I want you to have the best, and Rafe Hawk is the right man for this project."

Something about Arthur's dogged persistence had troubled her then, and the American's presence disturbed her now. He made no attempt to hide his displeasure at the situation. Working on her project angered him for reasons she couldn't begin to fathom.

Something about the man unsettled her. He stirred feelings she didn't trust.

It struck her now that Arthur had cleverly sidestepped her previous attempts to discover his reasons for bringing in *this* architect. He'd claimed only that Rafe could fulfil everything she ever dreamed of with the project. Not for the first time Trudi wondered what made Rafael Hawk so special.

"He's a man with vision," Arthur had enthused at the time. "He can take a person's dreams and bring them to life." And of course her brother knew about her dreams. Trudi had bartered those dreams, of making the residents' twilight years secure, as a trade-off for accepting the obligation of an inheritance she'd never wanted.

The sound of Arthur's voice impinged on her thoughts. "There will be no disputes over the inheritance of this place. I can guarantee that."

~*~

"Trudi, I'm sorry to interrupt, dear, but Bella needs you." Her newest resident, Judy Strathallan entered the library and hesitated before crossing to her side. "She's beginning to feel cold and wants to return to her room." She glanced at the two men then toward the French windows. "She doesn't want to meet any strangers. Can you persuade them to wait in the snug while we get her upstairs?"

"I can do better than that Judy," Trudi said in an undertone. "I'll send them both out to the site. Hopefully it won't take long."

"No, indeed. What's Arthur doing here so close to his wife's due date?" Judy asked, before adding, "I'll tell Bella you'll come in a moment."

"Thank you, Judy." Turning to Arthur, she rested her hand on his arm. "I'm afraid I can't do anything about the chalets right now, and I don't know how long I may keep you waiting. Perhaps it's better if you go home to Serena. You should be with her, you know, not hanging around here.

"I will reimburse Mr Hawk for his inconvenience today. I'm sure he'll understand." She risked a quick glance in Rafe's direction in time to see anger spark in those smoky eyes. What riled the man now?

Whatever. Bella needed her, and Trudi refused to pander to Rafe Hawk and his personal tantrums.

Arthur understood—no one, and nothing, came before Bella. His taciturn friend didn't need to know anything beyond the fact Trudi wanted him gone. She refused to feel guilty. She'd find someone else to design and oversee the construction of her chalets.

"No need for that," Arthur said. "What do you say if I show him around the area instead?"

Trudi glanced in Rafe's direction in time to see his frown deepen. Why agree to this commission if he didn't want it?

"Arthur, go home to Serena and take your friend with you. I don't anticipate enough spare time to deal with the chalets for the foreseeable future. Bella needs me, and I don't know—"

"Honey, I'm sorry. I understand how hard this is for you, but Rafe's returning to The States in a couple of days. Perhaps I can take him over to the site. If you have a spare moment when he's done, we can talk then." Arthur placed his arm around her shoulder and pulled her close for a hug. "Go. Leave this with me and Rafe. Give Bella a hug from me."

Trudi's concern for her friend overrode any desire to fight over the issue of the chalets. Wordlessly, she nodded and squeezed his arm, silently accepting his support. Then she left the room without acknowledging Rafe's presence.

She didn't understand his anger and didn't intend to let it get to her. If he wanted to leave, the sooner the better for her. Brushing him from her mind, she headed outside to join Bella.

The sound of the men's voices faded as they headed off in the other direction toward the projected site for the chalets.

"Judy says Arthur's brought his architect friend." Bella's anxiety reflected in her eyes.

"Yes."

"And?"

"And nothing. It's obvious the man's here under duress. I'm expecting him to turn the commission down." Trudi scooped Bella up into her arms.

"Why?"

"I don't know." Trudi sighed. "I can tell you you'll be scorched by his red-hot anger if you stand too close to him."

Making her way up the central staircase rising from the main hall, Trudi headed along the wide left-hand corridor and stopped to inhale deeply before entering Bella's room. The last time she'd been the recipient of so much anger, veiled or otherwise, Trudi had been running for her life.

Ohmigod! Where did that memory come from?

Before she managed to retain it, the fragment slipped into the mists of her forgotten past.

CHAPTER 3

"She's right, Arthur, you should be with Serena right now, not swanning around here sorting out another woman's problems when your wife might need you by her side quickly."

"Yes, you're right, I should," Arthur replied shortly. "So let's get moving." He walked across to the den and out the single glass door then turned right and away from the front of the house. "Trudi never asks for anything from anyone, and I mean to fulfil the first stage of this dream before we leave here today. Serena agrees with this, so let's not waste any more time arguing."

Moving briskly Arthur led the way through a small glade of sun-dappled trees. When they reached the other side of the coppice, Rafe marvelled at the field full of blooming wildflowers in front of them. At one side a narrow, crystal-clear stream burbled gently over a stony bed. A small bridge led to an area beyond, where someone had removed the topsoil and levelled the ground. The scene reminded him of the famous blue willow pattern on his mother's china.

"Damn the woman, I told her I would do that for her!"

Unsure if Arthur's hissing words were meant for his ears, Rafe didn't respond. Instead he asked, "Aren't they rather a long way from the main house if these chalets are for the elderly resident and one of them needs help?"

He looked back and realized another short path lead directly back to the main building. Obviously Arthur brought him here by the scenic route. Several windows overlooked the levelled ground, and he detected movement at one of them. Silently, he conceded the site was more ideal than he'd first estimated.

"Trudi wants these chalets for the more active, independent residents so they can maintain a home environment, keep their privacy, and still be close enough," Arthur said. "She intends to build in blocks of three."

"That's hardly an economical way to undertake a project of this sort. If she builds the twelve at once, she'll get better discounts for her materials. She must have buildings and barns she can store them in."

"She's not prepared to overextend herself, even if it's going to cost her more." Arthur sighed. "I've explained this to her. Endlessly. Still she refuses to budge on the issue.

Even Serena's failed to persuade her. Serena's hoping once the project has started, Trudi will accept our offer of a loan."

"She appears to lack basic business acumen," Rafe retorted, before striding across the tiny bridge. "We'll need to widen and strengthen this for the safety of her residents. I suggest doubling the width. More importantly where do the trucks bring in the materials?"

"Over there."

Arthur pointed toward the continuation of the broad sweeping driveway. It ran in front of the Hall and curved round the glade they'd come through before closing in on the levelled ground. It wouldn't take much work to connect the site to the driveway access. Silently, Rafe acknowledged Trudi chose the spot well.

Her residents would be close enough for any assistance to reach them promptly. Yet they'd retain their privacy. They'd create a community within a community. While the plan didn't begin to resemble the prestige of the senior communities in the U.S., it had its own charm. He visualized the houses bathed in evening sunlight, the people moving about in their gardens, the sound of contented conversation drifting on a gentle breeze.

Arthur's voice abruptly dispelled the vision. "Do you need my help to hold equipment or anything?"

❧❧❧

Perched on the window seat in Bella's room for more than an hour, Trudi watched the two men below, walking about the site as the sun crossed the sky. Their movements reminded her of a surreal ballet where the dancers danced to the sound of nature's song. They measured and discussed, before changing positions and measuring some more. She didn't recognize the equipment Rafe used, but every time she glanced down at the scene, the two men were deeply involved in their work. They'd removed their shirts. Arthur's pale skin, the result of too many hours in the office these days, glistened in the sun. His slender frame belied his natural strength.

Much to his boss's disappointment, Arthur gave up field operations when Serena announced her pregnancy. He'd advertised his intention to stay home for his children as they grew up. Having lost their parents at sixteen, Trudi understood Arthur's need to be around for his own as they grew up.

He'd make wonderful a father. After all, she'd given him plenty of practice. Her lips curved in a reminiscent smile. He'd been a wonderful brother to her in her times of need.

She watched Rafe Hawk move to the far side of the site and bend low to hammer in a small peg taken from the back pocket of jeans slung low on his narrow hips—jeans in danger of exposing his neat derriere.

Well-toned muscles rippled under the sun-kissed skin on his wide shoulders and back.

She watched him straighten, turn and call across to Arthur, and she sensed a frisson of recognition flow through her system like molten liquid.

How could a man who'd not bothered to hide his contempt for her ignite the feeling she'd known him in another lifetime?

Nothing made sense. What possible connection did she have with the disdainful American?

Unable to find answers to any of her queries she looked away from the scene below, and with a sigh, glanced over her shoulder to ensure Bella still slept. Her heart clenched at the injustice soon to deprive her of her dearest friend. Kind, generous Bella didn't deserve to battle terminal cancer. Biting down on her inner lip, Trudi fought against the dread clogging her throat, the fear she wouldn't cope when Bella's sweet smile faded forever. That she wouldn't be good enough for Bella's daughter, Lizzie.

"Trudi?" Bella's tired, reedy voice disturbed the silence.

"I'm here." Moving to sit on the edge of the bed Trudi lifted Bella's hand and gently rubbed her thumb across the translucent skin. "What can I do for you, hon?"

"I'd like to talk to Vince. Will you tell him I need to see him now and not this evening?"

"Of course I will." Tenderly, Trudi brushed a strand of hair away from her friend's face, pressed the speed dial on her cell phone and waited.

She tried to imagine how she'd cope if faced with the knowledge she wouldn't live to see Rachel grow up and found she couldn't. She wondered if Bella's extraordinary strength of character came from her acceptance of an inevitability she couldn't change?

Trudi remembered Judy saying, when you stared death in the face your priorities fell into place. And Judy, like all her other residents, knew about staring death in the face.

Judy had shifted in her chair that day. "Before he gave up field work when your sister-in-law fell pregnant again, I worked on several Ops with Arthur. He's a good man to have at your back. I'm glad he's there for Vincent. It hit Vincent hard when they diagnosed Bella's cancer this time."

The sound of logs settling in the grate had filled the silence.

"It's so unfair." The words escaped before Trudi could muzzle them.

For five years Bella had battled cancer. Twice they'd celebrated when they believed she'd gone into remission, and despaired when it returned a third time, crying when the Doctors gave their final prognosis. Together she and Bella had railed against the cruel fate soon to separate them, and they'd clung to each other through their fear of the future.

No way would they have coped without the wonderful support and regular visits from the hospice staff and MacMillan nurses who'd supported Bella's decision to stop the treatments. Trudi swallowed the tears threatening to choke her.

People often assumed, because of her tranquillity, Bella lacked strength. They couldn't have been more wrong.

"Did you get through to him?"

Bella's voice brought Trudi back to the moment. She bent forward and gently brushed her finger along the drawn skin on Bella's face.

"Not yet, but he'll come when Heather contacts him."

Bella's lips moved in a travesty of her former smile. "I'd like to come downstairs, before he arrives, Trudi. Will you help me?"

"Of course. I'll get your wrap for you. Which one would you like?"

Trudi had bought several fashionable wraps when Bella's condition deteriorated, hoping the pretty colors and feminine designs would cheer her up.

"The gold one, please. It reminds me of warm sunny days, and I want to look good for Vince."

ᕲᕲᕲ

Before Trudi lifted her off the bed, Bella raised her hand. "I want to talk to you before the girls come home. After all, it's the last day of term, and we won't have much opportunity during their summer break."

Holding the golden wrap over one arm, Trudi perched on the edge of the bed. "What's so important you can't talk in front of them?"

"Do you remember the day they were born?"

"Not a day I'm likely to forget," Trudi agreed with a wry smile. "The doctors predicted their arrivals two weeks apart. Lizzie couldn't wait and arrived a week early. And Rachel decided to arrive a week late. We ended up in the same birthing room together because of the dreadful motorway pile-up. The hospital staff was on high alert, and they ran out of beds up in the wards."

"And when Lizzie emerged, you nearly delivered her before the midwife arrived, even though Rachel was clamouring for attention at the time, too."

"As I said." Trudi smiled. "Not a day easily forgotten."

"You saved Lizzie's life. You saved mine." Bella's hand skittered over the bed covers, and Trudi lifted it gently into hers. "If I remember, the midwife didn't even have time to get you back onto the bed before Rachel arrived."

"True. Ten years down the line, I don't mind admitting how scared I was for both of us, for *all* of us." She couldn't remember experiencing such relief as the moment she heard the midwife's hurried footsteps approaching their room.

"Lizzie looks on you as her second mother, so please, don't fear the future."

Once again, Bella's ability to tune into her thoughts and fears astounded Trudi. "I won't deny there's fear there. Anger's a natural part of grieving, and I'll be her nearest target. I admit I'm afraid I won't be enough for her." She couldn't believe she'd just spilled her fears to her friend who had problems enough of her own.

"Vince will bring various legal documents with him for you to sign." Before she could object, Bella continued. "You have always been there for me and Lizzie. And I can't think of a better way of expressing my heartfelt love for you and your friendship. Knowing Lizzie will be safe in your care means everything to me. I know," she continued, her voice fading fast. "It's as hard for you as me. In some ways, probably harder."

Trudi wanted to protest. What could be harder than losing your options to choose? But she bit back the words when her phone chirped.

"He's not in his office," Heather, Vince's secretary explained. "He's trying to catch Arthur before he goes off on paternity leave."

"Arthur's here," Trudi told her. "Please will you page Vince? Bella wants to see him this afternoon."

"Thank you," Bella whispered. The gray pallor had long since chased away the pink and creamy tones of her skin.

"An English Rose," Vince used to call his sister, much to Bella's disgust.

"Far better an English Rose, than a Bean Pole," Trudi used to respond with a laugh.

⌘⌘⌘

"That's flying low." Rafe looked up at the sound of an approaching helicopter. "Do they always fly this low over here?"

Shielding his eyes from the sun, Arthur squinted at the chopper. "No. I imagine that's Vince."

"Vince? Do you mean your boss? He knows you're on leave, right? So why's he coming here?" Rafe retrieved his shirt and discarded jacket and closed his pad before stuffing it in his shirt pocket.

"Bella." Without breaking stride, Arthur snatched up his own shirt and began running back to the Hall, leaving Rafe to follow in his wake.

"Who's Bella?" Rafe asked as they reached the French doors. "And why is she so important the head of your national security flies down here?"

"Bella is Vince's sister, and I presume she asked Trudi to call him." Briefly, without slowing his pace, Arthur explained why Trudi had dropped everything to go to Bella's side when she'd called earlier.

The whine of the rotor blades faded, replaced by a melody of cheerful birdsong. They reached the house in time to see Vince stride across the library and disappear into the hall. On his way he dropped his dark- gray, pinstriped jacket across the surface of Trudi's huge desk.

Not knowing what to say, Rafe silently followed Arthur through the open French doors. He'd made no secret of his contempt for Trudi. Now her instant dismissal of the chalet project and genuine concern for Bella showed a side to the woman Rafe hadn't expected.

He wanted to discover how many layers covered the truth behind the real Trudi Delaney before he left. And then he wondered why it mattered.

He found Arthur and Vince in the hall, their heads bent toward each other while they talked quietly.

"…children." Vince started moving toward the central stairway. "Is Trudi upstairs?"

"We returned to the house when you flew in, but I imagine so."

Leaning his shoulder against the doorjamb, Rafe watched the two men now deep in quiet conversation. To all outward appearances, in spite of the sweat beading Arthur's brow, they looked like a couple of normal business executives. Their natural air of authority and confidence commanded automatic respect from those around them. Few would suspect how, until recently, both men spent many years as undercover agents, nationally and internationally, in their country's secret service.

Arthur had introduced him to Vince when Rafe had sought Arthur's help after surviving the attempt on his life eleven years ago. It hadn't taken Vince long to discover Daniel Kinsale's other bastard son—one prepared to kill to ensure he inherited the Kinsale fortune and estates.

Startled out of his thoughts by the slam of a car door and running feet, Rafe watched two young girls hurtle through the open front door. One with raven-dark hair ran straight to Vince. The other, with honey blonde hair that glistened in the slanting beams of sunlight drifting through the far windows, took a running leap into Arthur's outstretched arms. Both girls reminded Rafe of his ten-year-old niece Tammy. The blonde's similarity to his niece took his breath away.

"Lizzie, is there a problem at school? You're not normally home for another couple of hours yet." Vince bent down to scoop his niece into his arms and kissed her soft cheek.

"Mrs. Taverham brought us back in her car." The blonde child landed a noisy kiss on Arthur's cheek.

"Is there trouble with the bus or something, Rachel?" Arthur slanted a glance at the child in his arms before looking toward the approaching figure of the girls' headmistress. "Hello Miss Taverham. It is good of you to take time out of your busy schedule to ferry the girl's home." With Rachel still in his arms, Arthur moved toward the silver-haired woman standing just inside the front door, his hand extended in greeting.

"Mr. Clifton. When she called me, Trudi told me you'd arrived unexpectedly." Miss Taverham clasped Arthur's hand in a firm grip. "I decided to bring the children home and save them the two-hour bus journey on this final day of the school term. If you have a moment, I would like a word with you while I'm here."

"Vince, I know you're anxious to see Bella." Arthur turned from Miss Taverham to Vince. "But will you take the girls to the kitchen for cookies and milk first? I'm not sure if Judy will be there at this time in the afternoon."

Before Vince moved, Miss Taverham placed a detaining hand on his arm. "I'd like to speak with you too, Mr. Parker, it won't take long. Can we go somewhere private?"

"If they're willing to come with me, I'm happy for the girls to show me the way to the kitchen." Rafe stepped away from the office door and moved toward the group in the hall.

As one, the group turned. Vince, the first to speak, moved toward Rafe, his hand outstretched. "Rafe, isn't it?" Rafe nodded, shaking Vince's hand. "How good to see you," Vince said. "It's been a long time. What brings you to Kinsale Hall?"

"It's good to see you too, Vince, but perhaps we better postpone our visit until later. If they'll agree to join me, I'm happy to stay with the girls," he offered again.

"This is my niece, Lizzie," Vince smiled at the girl still in his arms. "Lizzie, this is Rafe Hawk, an old friend."

"Hello." She offered a shy smile before emulating her uncle and holding out her hand.

With a warm smile, Rafe held the small hand in his, carefully shaking it. "I'm pleased to meet you, Lizzie, and will be happy to escort you both to the kitchen for cookies and milk," he replied, holding the child's scrutiny and waiting for her decision. He got on well with his niece Tammy, but would these girls feel secure enough to go with him?

"This is my friend and sister Rachel." Lizzie indicated the honey-blonde child now holding Arthur's hand.

Rafe bent on one knee, keeping his eyes level with Lizzie's friend, "Hello Rachel, it's not everyday a man's introduced to two such beautiful girls at once." He extended his hand and waited.

Rachel giggled nervously, casting a brief glance at Arthur before placing her hand in his and smiling. "Thank you, but can we go and see Bella first?"

"Your mum is with Bella, sweetheart," Arthur responded.

"Please, we want to go to Bella first."

Rafe noticed Vince's frown and tried to imagine his emotions right now. Split between his need to visit his sister and his instinctive manners toward the children's teacher, would he agree to Rachel's request to visit Bella?

Lizzie turned in his arms. "Please," she whispered.

"Mummy told us this morning she wants to see you, but please can we go up while you talk with Miss Taverham? Then we'll go with your friend to get cookies."

Over Lizzie's shoulder, Rafe met Vince's questioning glance before directing his gaze in Arthur's direction. With a brief nod, Rafe turned and took Lizzie from Vince's arms.

Undercurrents he didn't understand flowed between the adults, and when he looked at the girls he recognized the same emotions reflected in their eyes. If the girls were the same age as Tammy they'd be ten years old, but the eyes that turned in his direction revealed wisdom beyond those of most children that age.

He remembered Arthur's words as they'd returned from the site. It seemed from his observations the children were fully aware of Bella's situation. How did a child cope with the knowledge? Lizzie called Rachel her friend and her sister. Did that mean Bella was the children's mother?

'*Rafe, you are so good with children. It's past time you had some of your own.*' His mother's words echoed in his head.

'*Only if they belong to someone else,*' he'd quipped right back at her.

He smiled at both girls and held out his hands. "May I escort you, ladies?"

Rafe tried to analyse his jumbled feelings and failed. In a space of a few hours he'd found himself in the one place he never wanted to set foot again. He'd met a woman who aroused emotions he didn't want to experience. Emotions he didn't understand, feelings of recognition beyond the explainable.

The women in his life expected him to leave their bed before dawn. They played by the rules. And yet he'd spent less than an hour in Trudi's company and felt certain the rules would fly out of the window if he pursued her.

Good Lord, where were these thoughts taking him? He felt himself hardening just thinking about her. He'd offered to look after the girls and couldn't keep his mind on track. Time he got his head into gear and north of his belt.

"In exchange for my escort, you can both act as my guide. How does that sound?"

"Thank you." Rachel turned to Lizzie. "Come on."

"What do we call you?" Lizzie had put her arms round Rafe's shoulders when Vince passed her over.

"Our mummies say it's rude to call a grownup by his first name."

"My niece calls me Uncle Rafe, but because I'm not your uncle, perhaps you better call me Rafe or, if your mother objects, then you can call me Mr. Hawk, or Hawk. I'll answer to both." He smiled down at the upturned faces. "Let's go and ask, shall we?"

CHAPTER 4

How did she get so lucky? Trudi watched her daughter race into the room and into her arms before planting a sloppy kiss on her cheek. She truly didn't know. Rachel's laughing silver-gray eyes were unlike hers. Trudi wondered again about her daughter's father and became lost in what memories she had.

ↄ৵ↄ৵

"Rachel doesn't have your eyes."

Judy's comment a few weeks after her arrival triggered questions Trudi couldn't answer.

How did you tell a comparative stranger you couldn't remember the man who'd fathered your child? "No, and she doesn't get them from my side of the family."

She'd hunched one shoulder and let it drop. For eleven years her dreams had turned to nightmares, fragmenting memories and blurring the line between fact and fiction. Who in their right mind admitted aloud to missing several hours, maybe days of their life?

And yet one afternoon while Bella slept and before the girls returned from school, she'd found herself doing just that.

They'd sat on the patio in the spring sunshine.

"You never talk of Rachel's father." Judy's half query, half statement hung in the air for several seconds before Trudi answered.

"That's because I don't remember him."

"Oh my! You don't mean someone spiked your drink, do you?"

"No, it's more complicated than that. The doctors say it's aggravated by what they call selective amnesia." Relief washed over her when Judy understood. She'd had to ask her doctor to explain why she'd lost the critical events between the poker game and asking for an early morning cup of coffee from a street vendor.

"How long a period does your amnesia cover?"

"They assessed it is between sixteen and thirty-plus hours."

"What's your last memory?"

"A poker game."

"Where?"

"At home."

"Your home?"

Trudi remembered her unease at Judy's question. How did she explain the house she'd lived in became her prison almost from the day she married Denny, against Arthur's advice. "He gambled."

"Who?"

"Denny, my husband. He'd go off for days at a time, and when he came home I always knew whether he'd won or lost by his mood."

"What does this have to do with Rachel's father?"

"You have to understand, Denny and I—we were—he didn't—He'd invite people to the house and they'd play cards late into the night."

"Did you play?"

"Me? Oh no. Normally Denny kept me away from his friends."

Judy shifted in her chair. "But the missing night's different?"

"Yes." The sun no longer warmed her skin. Trudi wrapped her arms around her waist in an effort to stop the chill seeping into her bones.

"Why?"

"They'd been playing for several hours when Denny called for me to join them."

"You said he kept you away."

"Normally, and I assumed it would be the same that night. But when I joined them, he made me stand behind

the visitor's chair. Not too close, you understand. I couldn't
see the man's face. I remember he seemed well built, and I
guessed he'd equal Denny's height, which would make him
around six feet tall, perhaps a couple of inches taller, I don't
know."

"Visitor, not friend?"

"Yes. Something I overheard during the afternoon
gave me the impression Denny had never met the man
before but held a grudge against him. I overheard Denny
boast about cleaning the bastard out."

"Did you know what he meant?"

"No. Not then, but I've often wondered since if it had
something to do with this place."

"Kinsale Hall?" Judy's astonishment shot her upright
in her chair.

"It didn't take me long, after the wedding to realize
what little Denny told me about himself amounted to a
pack of lies. I do know, because, Jason, one of his body-
guards, told me Denny never met his father but always
claimed his father was the previous owner of the Hall.
When the old Lord Kinsale died, the executors searched for
the rightful heirs and when they couldn't find them, Denny
got his greedy hands on the place. It didn't do him any
good. The terms of the old Lord's will didn't leave much
loose change, and Denny couldn't raise funds against the
property. Don't ask me to explain the details because I
haven't a clue." The words kept coming—secrets she'd
never shared before, not even with Arthur. Judy asked, and
the answers popped out of her mouth. Trudi wanted to

stop spewing out her soul, but the words refused to remain silent.

"So you moved in here with Denny?"

"No."

"Oh. Go on."

"Where was I?"

"Standing behind the stranger's chair."

"Right. They'd been drinking during the afternoon and evening. I remember the whiskey bottles and beer cans littering the floor. The room had one overhead light bulb above the table and you could hardly see through the haze of cigar and cigarette smoke. They'd obviously ordered pizzas because they'd chucked the boxes and leftovers on the floor, too."

"Yuk!"

"Quite." Trudi smiled at Judy's disgust. "When I entered the room, I knew things were not going Denny's way."

"Go on."

"The stranger had a pile of money in front of him, and the tick beneath Denny's right eye kept twitching. Anyone who knew Denny understood that meant trouble, but the stranger either didn't notice the signs or ignored them. The more impassive the stranger remained the higher Denny's anger spiked."

"How long were you there?"

"I don't know. Several hours."

"Did you know the other players? Were they winning?"

"They were Denny's security men, and they were losing too."

"Your memory seems clear enough so far. What happened next?"

"I remember the stranger's watch glinting in the light. It looked 'designer.' He called his bid, and then Denny staked me—"

"What! Your husband staked you? What happened next?"

"I can't remember." Trudi dropped her head into her hands, dragged in a deep breath, and then another to keep the infringing darkness at bay.

"Nothing? You remember nothing from then until when?"

Trudi looked into Judy's face and away. "The next true memory is of ordering a coffee at one of these street vendors and him cussing at me for handing him a twenty pound note."

"And then?"

"I grabbed the money back and ran. When I stopped running I discovered my feet were bare, and I wore a man's blue silk shirt tied with a narrow brown leather belt. I don't know where the money came from, but I remember reaching into the shirt pocket for it."

"So you are missing the hours between your husband staking you in the card game late one night and you ordering a coffee early one morning?"

Trudi rose and began pacing.

"The following morning, or the next one?" Judy prompted when Trudi remained silent.

"No one knows."

"And what do you remember about the stranger apart from what you've already mentioned?"

Pausing in her pacing, Trudi stabbed at the air. "I don't know."

"So you remember something?"

"I have dreams. I can no longer separate the facts from the fiction."

Trudi slumped into the nearest chair, rested her elbows on her knees, and steepled her fingers. With deliberate care she leaned her chin on her fingertips and gazed straight ahead. "They're jumbled. Sometimes I dream of Denny's dogs baying behind me. Other times I hear rushing water and darkness, noise and silence that go hand in hand with people and lights."

"Are you alone?" Martha leaned forward.

"I don't know, but I don't think so."

"If you're not alone, who do you think is with you?"

"That's impossible to say, but you have to remember I hadn't set foot outside the house since right after the wedding."

Judy's sharp intake of breath reached Trudi where she sat. "How long…"

"Five years." Trudi dropped her hands between her knees and studied her listener's obvious shock. She wanted to ask Judy to stop her questioning, but the words refused to come.

"How did you get out, if, as you say, you remember rushing water?"

"I don't know that either."

"Can you be sure Denny isn't Rachel's father?"

"Wrong blood group. His blood group was A-Positive, mine is A-Negative, and Rachel's is type O."

"How come you're living at Kinsale Hall?"

"Arthur and Vince came to an accord with the lawyers dealing with the estate. They officially leased the Hall on government business"

"Surely, as his widow, you'd inherit from Denny?"

"I refused to accept it. It didn't seem right to me."

"So how come you're here, and why do you call yourself Delaney instead of Cadmore?"

"I changed my surname by deed pole to my mother's maiden name. And I came here as part of Arthur and Vince's deal with the lawyers. They insisted I became the landlady, for want of a better way of describing my position here. In reality, they wanted me and Bella to move here with the girls so they could keep an eye on us."

Judy's laughter mingled with Trudi's.

⁂

"Mummy, you're not listening!"

Rachel's demanding tones penetrated Trudi's memories and shot her back to the present and Bella's room. "Mrs. Taverham is talking to Uncle Arthur and

Uncle Vince. Can we go and get some cookies with Mr Hawk?"

A warm tingling sensation prickled up her neck. Trudi lifted her gaze from her daughter's laughing face to the man leaning against the doorjamb.

Shock ripped through her. Of course, that would explain the sudden recall of Judy's conversation. His attitude mirrored that of the stranger she'd just been thinking about a moment ago. It certainly hadn't been sympathy she'd seen in his eyes.

What then?

Shock? Yes. Compassion? Definitely not! Disgust? Absolutely. Revulsion? It would seem so. Contempt? Why?

Why would a stranger hold her in such obvious contempt and still agree to design the chalets? Perhaps he hadn't. Perhaps he'd only agreed to consider the project for his friend and would find an excuse to turn the commission down before he and Arthur left.

Stifling a gasp as awareness ripped through her, she dropped her gaze and nestled her face against her daughter's soft rosy cheek.

"How did school go today, and how come you're home early?" she asked, not prepared to acknowledge Rafe Hawk's presence. Let him add bad manners to his contempt of her.

Why should she care? She didn't want to examine her feelings toward him. Experiencing any kind of reaction for him beyond the normal acceptance she would give to any friend of Arthur's sent shock waves coursing through her.

She didn't need the extra burden of admitting to emotions she vowed she'd never entertain again.

She certainly didn't want to care for anyone beyond those around her right this moment. Rachel. Lizzie and Bella. Arthur, his wife Serena, and even Vince had managed to sneak into her affections. She had no room in her heart for anyone else and no desire to make room either, apart from Serena's new baby when it came.

"How was school today?" Trudi asked again, deciding to ignore Rachel's request.

"Okay. Miss Taverham brought us home because she wanted to talk to Uncle Arthur and Uncle Vince."

"He asked us to tell you he'll come up in a moment, Mum," Lizzie said. Trudi studied Lizzie lying on the bed beside her mother, their fingers twined together.

"Did she say why she wanted to see your uncles?" Trudi asked.

What could be so important to bring the girl's headmistress out here on the last day of the summer term? She hoped the woman didn't keep the men too long. Her gaze strayed to the man propping up the doorjamb. Why did he stand there, neither in nor out of the room? Surely he realized this wasn't the time or place to hang around in condemnation of her or anyone else in the house?

"I promised to take the girls down to the kitchen and give them their milk and cookies." Rafe's gaze never shifted from her face.

Blast the man. Did he include mind-reading as part of his curriculum vitae? "Believe me, the girls can locate the kitchen on their own and are more than able to find the cookie jar." Valiantly, Trudi fought the smile tugging at the corner of her lips. She refused to break eye contact first. For some reason he seemed determined to get a rise out of her.

"Ah, but the girls have agreed to an exchange—their guidance for my escort to the cookie jar and milk jug." The corners of his mouth lifted in a half grin that reached her solar plexus with the impact of an Exocet Missile.

Forget the challenge, she decided, swiftly glancing across to Bella. Had she or Lizzie seen the exchange? Fortunately Rachel missed it. Otherwise, she'd pepper Trudi with questions. Generally quieter than Lizzie, once Rachel latched onto a query, she never let go until she received an answer that satisfied her.

"Forgive me, but have we met before?" The sound of Bella's voice snapped Trudi's attention back to her friend. Bella stared the man standing in the doorway. "If so, I don't remember when, but you seem vaguely familiar."

"No ma'am, I don't believe we've met before." Rafe moved toward the bed and laid his hand on the covers near Bella's. Trudi noticed he moved his hand beneath Bella's and gently folded his fingers lightly around hers.

What had caught Bella's attention? Trudi's gaze swung from Rafe Hawk back to her friend. A puzzled frown etched Bella's face. What bothered her about the man sitting beside her?

Trudi opened her mouth to speak then snapped it shut again and continued to weigh up the newcomer. Had she met the man before? If so, how come she didn't recognize him? She'd ask Bella later what had disturbed her about Rafe.

"I'm a friend of Arthur's. I've come to assess Ms. Delaney's project for the chalets." Rafe swept his free hand in Trudi's direction.

"I'm Bella Munroe, and this is my daughter Lizzie." She turned her loving gaze to the child lying beside her, careful not to cuddle too close to her mother. Bella raised her hand and gently caressed her daughter's cheek.

"It's a pleasure to meet you ma'am, I only wish circumstances were different. When they're ready, I'm happy for the girls to escort me to the kitchen." Laughter lines fanned out from his eyes as he returned Bella's smile, encompassing Lizzie at the same time.

"That sounds like a good idea from where I'm standing."

"Vince!" Wreathed in smiles, Bella turned to her brother now standing where Rafe had been only a few moments earlier.

"How's my best girl?" He moved to the bed and bent down to brush his lips across his sister's forehead.

Rafe took up his stance against the doorframe again to give Vince more room.

"Thanks for coming." Bella indicated the bed and watched her brother sit on the edge near her shoulder before resting his arm along the headboard behind her.

He looked out of place against her pale pink sheets with ivory white ruffles on the matching pillow-cases and at the same time managed to appear completely at ease and relaxed. The late afternoon sun burnished his burnt-toffee-brown hair and revealed the shadows beneath his eyes. He'd lost his jacket and tie and released the top buttons of his starkly-white shirt.

"I'll go and get the den ready for you, hon." Trudi moved away from her perch against the window sill, where she'd enjoyed the warmth of the late afternoon sun on her back.

"No, don't go." Bella turned to her. "Vince and I have something we want to discuss with you." She turned to Vince. "Have you brought everything with you?"

"Yes, Belle, I've seen to everything and have the documents with me," he replied, laying a blue folder on top of her bed covers. Turning to Trudi he added, "Please stay." A smile softened his normally-severe features.

ↄ乃ↄ乃

After her discussions with Vince and Bella, Trudi spent the rest of the afternoon and evening moving Bella's things from her room down to the den. She'd shifted her own books and art paper into the library-cum-office-study, where she'd organise them later. Now she smoothed the duvet and turned back the corner ready for when Vince carried his sister downstairs.

What right did she have to indulge in a pity-party? Trudi asked herself. Nothing Bella and Vince said this afternoon compensated for the imminent loss of her friend. She'd failed to dissuade either of them from changing their minds and found herself signing documents and deeds for a property to ensure security for Lizzie, Rachel, and herself for the rest of their lives. Tears stung the back of her eyelids. Nothing equalled the value of Bella's unconditional friendship.

Vince had added his own gratitude to Bella's when Trudi had agreed months ago to legally adopt Lizzie. And for a few months now, Lizzie was in the unusual position of having two legal mothers.

Guilt swept through Trudi, swift, sharp and cutting. More painful than any knife Denny had used on her. She heard someone's keening moans, unaware they were hers until Arthur's arms held her safely against his chest. His hand cupped the back of her head, encouraging her to lean on his strength and rest her cheek on his shoulder.

"I know, hon. I know." His whispered words unlocked the sobs she'd held inside for so long. They wracked her body and robbed her legs of the strength to remain upright. His lips brushed the top of her head, and he pushed a large hanky into her hands.

Her tears refused to stop. "Did Vince tell you why Bella wanted him to come today?"

"Yes. He spoke with me some time ago when Belle first discussed the idea with him and asked me whether I thought you would agree. He anticipated your reaction but knows how much Bella needed you to accept. You deserve it."

"How can you say that?" She glared at him through her tears. "And if you knew Bella intended to leave me the farm, why insist I agree to the solicitors' request to accept the responsibility of this place? And what about the chalets? Why let me go ahead with them?" She swiped the back of her hand across her eyes. "I'm sorry. I don't expect any answers now. And I didn't mean to rain all over you. Thank you."

With a swift hug and peck on her forehead, Arthur stepped away. "When they come downstairs, I'll ask Vince and Rafe to help us re-arrange the library."

"Can't we move everything between us? Shall we try before calling on Vince? We don't need your friend either." Silence met her words. If she'd hoped to provoke a comment about Rafe from her brother, her attempt failed. "If we move the desk over to the opposite wall, we can put the bed where the desk is now."

"It's too close to the window," Arthur responded after a brief pause. "We don't want you getting a chill. How about we leave the desk and move the sideboard to the opposite wall? Then when you place your Z-bed there, you will have a clear view into the Den. And during the night, you'll face no obstructions if you have to get up in the dark."

Trudi studied the room with Arthur's suggestion in mind. The bookshelves on two walls, from polished wooden floor to panelled ceiling, dominated the room, and the scarred mahogany chest under discussion weighed a ton. Considering his idea, she pinched the bridge of her nose.

On reflection, his plan made sense. She could always move her Z-bed into the den nearer to Bella later.

⁓⁓⁓

Rafe watched with growing disapproval when Vince crossed his sister's room to wrap his arms around Trudi and kiss her cheek before joining Bella. How many men did the woman need fawning over her to satisfy her ego?

He'd noticed Vince glance in his direction over Trudi's shoulder and couldn't understand the challenge he saw in the other man's eyes. Why on earth would Vince imagine he, Rafe, cared who kissed, cuddled, and hugged Trudi? He watched the children's reactions when so many men wrapped themselves around Trudi and was astonished by their obvious acceptance and love. Weird!

Whatever the situation, he needed to make tracks for home, but again, the state of affairs at the Hall delayed him. He couldn't take the car and leave Arthur without transport if Serena went into labour. The sound of Arthur's voice calling him from the book-lined study disturbed his thoughts.

With a sigh, he headed in Arthur's direction and hoped his friend would soon decide to put his wife before the woman who behaved like his mistress.

"How's Serena?" Rafe asked. "Have you heard from her recently?"

"I can't stay much longer." Arthur kept his voice low. "Serena's contractions have started. She's insisting she's still okay, but I'll have to leave soon. First, I need to get this heavy stuff moved."

"If that's the case, why are you still here?" Rafe demanded roughly, unable to keep his own voice low.

"Arthur?" Trudi joined them in the hall. "Did you say Serena's contractions have started? For goodness sake, why are you still here? We can manage."

"I'll just—"

The shrill of his mobile phone interrupted him before he could respond. "Serena? What! I'm on my way." He turned to Trudi, "I'm sorry, hon, I have to go." He gave her a bear hug before heading for the door.

"What's going on?"

Everyone turned toward the stairs to see Vince carrying Bella in his arms.

"Serena—The baby—It's on its way. I have to go."

"I'll get my coat and drive you to the hospital." Rafe headed toward the pile of discarded jackets still draped over the desk in the library.

"Use the chopper, Arthur. Max will take you to the hospital and come back for me tomorrow. Go on man." Vince spoke across Rafe as Arthur hesitated.

"Give her a hug from me." At Bella's reedy request, Arthur turned, came back, and brushed her waxen cheek with a gentle caress of his lips. "Love you," he whispered.

"Bye." A tear slipped silently down Bella's cheek.

But Arthur didn't notice. He'd already rushed off toward the waiting helicopter.

A few moments later, the rising sound of engine and rotor-whine filled the house. The helicopter's lights flashed across the windows, filling the room with brilliant white before swinging away. The sound faded into the failing summer evening.

"I'll drive Arthur's car back for him when I've helped shift the chest for Trudi." Rafe headed for the library only to be halted by Vince's request that he not leave before they'd talked.

"Later." Vince said before passing Rafe and carrying Bella into the den.

❧❧❧

Leaning back on the patio lounger, Rafe welcomed the warm breeze ruffling his hair. He rested his head against the cushions and watched the stars wink and twinkle as first one then another, followed by several more, scattered across the velvety blue sky.

He studied one and wished he could simply jump into Arthur's car and drive away from the memories this place invoked. If Vince hadn't briefly left his sister's bedside to explain that if he was called he had to have transport back to his office now he'd lent his helicopter to Arthur, Rafe would've left long ago.

"Wait for me," Vince had asked quietly before returning to sit with Bella.

Rafe sipped the coffee Trudi had brought out to him a while ago. Stopping only long enough to make certain it was how he liked it, she'd wordlessly retraced her steps. If he leaned forward, he could see her sitting at her desk, occasionally writing something on a piece of paper or entering information into some book while she steadily worked through the pile of paperwork he'd seen on the desk-top when they'd arrived.

The soft murmur of voices filtered through the open French doors, not loud enough for him to make out the words, but distinguishable enough for him to realize several different people sought Trudi out during the couple of hours he'd relaxed on the patio.

For a while he watched her shadow moving over the paving slabs when she rose to pace back and forth in her office. He found it difficult to equate the insight of the hard-working woman in the study with the siren who'd wrapped herself around his friend on their arrival.

Would the real Trudi please stand up? Only a rustling sound in the nearby bushes responded to his question. In the distance a fox howled, and an owl screeched.

The sound of hushed voices carried on the still evening air. He recognized Trudi's. She must have moved closer to the open doors.

"…said it wouldn't be long now. Can't you reschedule your work agenda?"

"I'll do what I can. But I still don't like leaving you alone at a time like this."

Rafe recognized Vince's equally low tones. He couldn't avoid hearing their conversation without reminding them of his presence. The only way off the patio was through the same French doors where Trudi and Vince appeared to be standing.

"Oh come on." The exasperation in Trudi's voice flowed across the still night air. "You, especially, cannot say I'm on my own. Tell me, who did all my residents work for before they came here? Could I be any better protected if you'd hired a platoon of SAS members?"

"It's not the same, Trudi, and you know it. I'm well aware how they feel about you, but they're not family. It's not the same," he said again.

"What exactly are you saying here, Vince?"

When Vince didn't respond, Rafe saw Trudi's shadow march across the slabs and back to the second figure silhouetted in the doorway.

"Apart from you who else can Bella call family?" she demanded. "I truly understand your predicament at work, but for God's sake Vince, surely they'll give you leave under the circumstances?"

Vince's shadow's hand reached up and fingered through his hair. "Trudi." He hesitated before continuing. "Let me ask him. Arthur wanted him to stay. He knew he would have to go back to Serena."

With a jerk, Rafe sat up straighter on the lounger. A sense of inevitability swept over him. Was this why Vince asked him to wait? He wished he'd ignored the man's request and taken Arthur's car and headed straight to Heathrow.

"Arthur's an old worry-wart, and you're fast catching up. I won't have it! If that makes me an ungrateful cow after everything you've both done for me—"

"Don't even go there, Trudi." Steel edged Vince's tone now.

Silence followed, and Rafe held his breath, afraid they'd discover his presence. "Take him back with you," she insisted. "If you don't, I'll send him back tomorrow. He's not family, and I don't want him here."

"You're not hearing me, Trudi. I'm not asking, I'm telling you. He's staying."

"He's agreed?" Trudi's sigh of defeat escaped through the gap in the French doors and landed in his lap. The stirring deep inside his belly wasn't anger. And if he'd interpreted the conversation correctly, he had every reason to be angry.

"Not exactly," Vince prevaricated.

"How 'not exactly?'" Rafe watched Trudi's shadow float over the patio slabs. "Are you telling me you haven't even asked him? How can you be sure he'll stay? You may not have noticed, but I can tell you he's already attempted to leave here at least twice, maybe more. Each time Arthur prevented him."

For the first time in his life, Rafe watched a shadow spin round. The silhouetted finger stabbed its companion on the chest.

"Are you telling me you and Arthur arranged this between you?" she demanded. "Next you'll tell me the three of you concocted this little story about him being an architect. He's one of your security guys, isn't he? You make me so mad.

"If you can't stay overnight, then I suggest you go collect your stooge and take him home with you. And if you are staying, then I suggest you sort out a spare room for him before you settle for the night. Whatever your decision, go away and let me get ready for bed."

Rafe watched the taller figure move to wrap his arms around his companion. "Don't get mad at us because we love you. I'll find Rafe and talk with him. Do you have any idea where he might be?"

"In the garden, relaxing on the lounger when I saw him last." Trudi stepped out of Vince's arms. Rafe watched Vince's shadow become a solid entity as he walked out onto the patio.

CHAPTER 5

With her arms wrapped around her legs and her chin resting on her knees, Trudi let the peace and tranquillity of her surroundings replace the resentment powering her emotions over the past week. The American's constant air of judgement stole her serenity.

A robin landed close by, his beady black eye on the food she'd scattered on the ground beyond her feet. With a quick tilt of his head, the cheeky orange-breasted bird watched the Greylag Geese approaching. Swift as a blink, the robin swooped, snatched a large piece of food, and flew off to a nearby willow branch.

Who had told Vince about the unidentified intruder?

When Trudi had first noticed someone watching the Hall, she'd taken care to conceal her discovery. She maintained her routine as closely as possible because of the girl's holidays. She took them shopping, visited the nearest MacDonald's, and had taken in a film they'd clamoured to see. Her residents' routines remained unchanged, sometimes joining the family for meals, at others choosing to use their own facilities.

What other reason did Vince have for foisting Rafe on her?

Every day, for the past week, Rafe took himself off, sometimes for the whole day, on others staying near the house, often inviting Lizzie and Rachel to accompany him on his outings. Wherever he went, he tramped through her mind twenty-four/seven. Whenever he approached her, the hairs on the back of her neck quivered.

He talked and smiled easily with her residents and the girls. But in her company he became monosyllabic and taciturn. His attitude bewildered her. If she truly believed it focussed on his forced prolonged stay, she could have tolerated the situation.

An impatient goose butted her hand demanding more food. Trudi laughed and spread her empty palms outwards and upwards in a gesture the fowl recognized. She laughed again when the closest goose seemed to huff its protest before heading back to the water. Another goose looked at her, its jet black eye gentle and inquisitive, before plopping down on the grass nearby and tucking its head beneath its wing.

Grateful for the undemanding company, Trudi let her thoughts skitter back over the past week. The longer Rafe stayed, the more time the girls spent with him. Begrudgingly, Trudi acknowledged his patience with them. At the same time, she didn't want the girls becoming too attached to the wretched man. But with luck he'd soon return home to his work.

With Bella's strength diminishing daily, the girls had enough to cope with, without getting too fond of someone who'd soon leave.

"Why am I not surprised to find you here?"

At the sound of Judy's laughing voice Trudi swivelled round, shielding her eyes with one hand, and met Judy's concerned gaze. In the six months Judy had been with them, she'd become like a second mother to Trudi.

"It looks so lovely I decided to take five minutes out before attacking the paperwork waiting for me."

"How long is he staying?" The jerk of Judy's head, toward the edge of the woods where Rafe and the children were disappearing into the shade of the trees, told Trudi whom she meant.

"Don't you like him?" Trudi patted the ground and watched the other woman settle beside her.

"There's something about him." Judy's shoulder hitched. "He's got secrets and more besides. I found him in the empty wing snooping through the old furniture and desks and things. My instincts tell me he's here for more than the contract to design your chalets."

"Vince asked him to stay on."

"He did?"

Under normal circumstances Trudi would have laughed at Judy's astonishment. The emotions Rafe stirred in Trudi disturbed her. She didn't have the time or inclination to discover why right now, and when he left it wouldn't matter.

"Why?" Judy swung round from watching the calmly floating geese on the water to study Trudi's face. "What's going on?" The comforting warmth of her hand on her arm soothed Trudi's jangled nerves. "Don't tell me it's nothing. Rafe's not the only one hiding something. What's worrying you, and have you spoken to Vince about it?"

Judy's hand on her arm prevented Trudi from avoiding her searching gaze.

"I don't know. No. I'm not sure, and no again." Trudi grinned before elaborating. "Vince never told me why he asked Rafe to stay. He's staying against his will, so Vince must have used some powerful argument to get him to remain here. What the reason is, neither Vince nor Rafe has told me. I'm sure it hasn't escaped your eagle eye Rafe holds me in contempt." Trudi glanced at her companion's face for confirmation. Yes, Judy had noticed Rafe's attitude toward her.

"What else is worrying you?" Judy asked, ignoring the opportunity to discuss their guest's attitude.

"This must remain between the two of us." Trudi shifted to face her friend. "I mean it. I don't want the children to learn about this, or for Bella to get wind of it. And it's none of Rafe's business."

"Tell me what's on your mind, and I'll tell you whether I agree to your terms." Judy smiled to soften her words.

"Someone's watching the Hall." Trudi waited for Judy to contradict her, to say she'd let her imagination run away with her.

"You've seen him, too?"

"Are you telling me you've been aware of this and not said anything? How long have you known?" Annoyance ripped through her before Trudi could school her features. "If you had any suspicions of strangers around here, you should've let me know. Especially now."

"Come on, Trudi. Give me a break. Surely you wouldn't expect someone who's been in surveillance as long as I have, to come to you before I'm sure of my facts?"

"No." Trudi sighed. "No. I'm sorry, you're right. I wouldn't. But thinking I've seen someone watching the place and having my fears confirmed is a bit unsettling." A sudden thought struck her. "Did you, by any chance, mention any of this to Vince last week when he visited Bella?"

"Of course I did. What else would you expect me to do when my old boss is handy?"

With a huff of exasperation Trudi swung herself onto her knees before standing, the nearby geese forgotten. She held out her hand and helped her companion to her feet. "Judy, do you mean to tell me you are responsible for Vince asking that obnoxious man to stay here? What have I ever done to you to deserve that?"

With a whimsical smile, she laced her hand in Judy's, and together they made their way back to the Hall.

⋐⋑⋐⋑

After reading to the girls and kissing them goodnight, Trudi headed for her office. The girls' growing attachment to Rafe concerned her. Why did he go out of his way to spend time them?

What kind of security clearance did he have to remain at the Hall? His friendship with Arthur and his agreement to remain here at the request of Vince, someone he hardly knew seemed odd. Or did it? She sifted through the little information she'd gathered about him. According to Arthur they'd known each other for years, but what about Vince? Had Rafe met Vince before arriving at Kinsale Hall? Upon reflection, Trudi decided the men knew each other better than they let on. Why else would Rafe allow Vince to coerce him into staying somewhere he plainly wished to leave?

Was Judy right? Did Rafe have some hidden agenda? Did he pump the girls for information about the residents? She'd never asked them, and their enthusiastic comments about Rafe covered only the activities they shared together. But they could easily give him information without knowing they did so.

Initially, both girls had held back in Rafe's company. But with each passing day, their eagerness grew as they accepted his requests to act as his guides and spent more and more time wandering around the grounds, exploring with him. In the evenings, they chattered to Bella about the different trees he'd shown them and how, a long time ago, logs were used to build houses. They also shared Rafe's stories about the log "cabins" he'd designed as holiday homes for famous film stars and other celebrities back home in The States.

A couple of nights ago, Trudi had listened to Rafe describe the log cabin he intended to build for himself. When the girls asked him what stopped him, he mentioned something about waiting for the right dream design. Trudi couldn't help wondering why he needed to wait. Surely the dream would evolve from the design? With a shrug she dismissed the thought.

He'd also taught the girls how to track different animals and how to assess the length of time since the creatures passed by. They'd followed some badgers tracks and come across their burrow then pestered Rafe to take them back in the evening to watch for the creatures emerging to forage. When Trudi unearthed his reasons for taking them on these exploratory expeditions, she'd send him packing. Especially if he was using them to cover his own ulterior motives.

The warmth of the smooth banister slid beneath her fingers. How many children over the years had rushed up the stairs, simply to slide down the banister again, filling the place with their laughter?

She remembered the girls' laughter when, with Bella at the top and herself at the bottom, both Rachel and Lizzie howled with joy as they repeatedly slid down the banister while she waited to catch them.

At the bottom of the stairs she turned right to check on Bella before settling down to the paperwork that never seemed to decrease. She didn't have time to dwell on Rafe's motives or her own lack of romance.

Now why had she included Rafe and love in the same thought?

Awareness of his male scent drifting across the hall thrummed through her senses, making a mockery of her assertion he had nothing to do with the butterflies fluttering in her stomach.

"Trudi?"

His voice reminded her of rich brown velvet caressing her skin and sent shivers of anticipation up her spine. She tried to remember the last time he'd approached her directly and failed.

"Yes?"

"If you have a moment, we have to talk." Rafe moved out of the shadow cast by the wide central stairway and walked beside her.

"Rafe, I realize you regret accepting Arthur's request to design the chalets. So I'm releasing you from any obligation and will reimburse you for your inconvenience." Unable to hide her resentment, she tried to soften her words with a smile.

"I don't want to talk about the chalets," he said. "Can we walk outside?"

Trudi followed when he led the way through the study and out the French doors to the patio. He chose the same path he and Arthur took one short week ago.

The descending sun set fire to the sky, warming the cold stonework of the Hall. Bats flittered past, the soft whisper of their flight hardly registering. She followed Rafe to the far side of the trees and stood looking over the levelled site.

"Why have you brought me here if you don't want to talk about the chalets?" This part of the estate always felt special to her. If anyone asked her to explain why, Trudi knew she couldn't put it into words. She looked into silver-gray eyes when Rafe turned to face her. His honey blond hair and sun kissed skin glowed in the setting sun. Again, she noticed the laugh lines fanning out from his eyes.

"Do you know why Vince asked me to stay on here?" Rafe leaned forward.

She felt the warmth of his breath feather against her cheek and shook her head, unable to speak for the sensations overwhelming her. His open shirt revealed his hard muscled chest, while the sharp tang of his aftershave tantalised her fantasies. Her heartbeat raced, reacting to a language she didn't comprehend. Surely no one in their right mind would give their heart to someone who displayed such contempt for her. Did that mean she'd lost her mind? With a huff of self-indignation, she tried to refocus her attention on Rafe's words. What had he said?

"Did he say anything to you before he left?"

"Who?" What had he asked her? She could lose herself in those shimmering silver- gray eyes. *Oh for heaven's sake,* she scolded herself, *get a grip, girl.*

"Trudi, have you listened a word I've said? It's important. Pay attention."

"Very well, Rafe, you've got my attention now. Did who tell me anything?" She responded with false diffidence.

"Vince. Did Vince tell you why he wanted me to stay on?"

"No, he did not," she snapped, annoyed with Vince for foisting this man on them. "Why do you ask?"

Rafe lowered himself onto the grass indicating Trudi follow suit.

"One of your residents shared her concern about an intruder lurking on and around the estate. She told Vince, and he asked me to stay on until he could find out more."

"I know Judy spoke to Vince. Until she told me this morning, I hadn't realized anyone else had spotted him."

"Are you saying you knew about the intruder and didn't say anything?" Rafe's cold and calculated voice startled Trudi faster than any raised, angry shouting.

"Vince may have asked you to stay around, but that doesn't give you the right to harangue me. Yes, I've seen someone hanging around on several occasions. But this is a large estate, and it could have been one of the many farm workers or visitors. Vince is a busy man with national security to deal with. I don't make it a habit to go running to him every time I have a little concern."

"You don't really expect me to believe that, do you?" Rafe snapped. "You're one of these women whose main delight is to have men hanging on your every whim. Why wouldn't you send for Vince or Arthur if you discovered a stranger trespassing?"

He couldn't have shocked her more if he'd punched her in the face. Fruitlessly, she tried to think back, wondering what she'd done to justify his attitude.

"You're entitled to your own opinion," she stated coldly. "But I don't have to stay here and listen to your insults."

Scrambling to her feet, she'd hardly straightened up before his strong lean fingers clamped round her wrist and pulled her down again. Losing her balance she landed in his lap, her face inches away from his.

"God, but I'm going to regret this," Rafe groaned.

Before she registered his words, his lips covered hers, crushing them against her teeth, bruising her soft flesh. His hand snaked round to the back of her head. His fingers tunneled through her hair, preventing her from avoiding his plundering tongue.

Bright flashes of light and splintering pain exploded in her head. Images too quick to hold onto flitted behind her eyes—images lost beneath the hungry force of Rafe's kiss.

His lips gentled and moved across her cheek then down the side of her neck. His hand pulled her shirt free and slipped beneath the soft material, leaving a quivering trail of need.

Nothing else mattered except the contact of his fingers on her skin. Her breasts ached for his hand to pay homage to them. Her lips mourned the loss of his as he lifted his face away from hers. She wanted him with a ferocity she'd never experienced before. Hands, ready a moment ago to shove him away, travelled of their own volition to sift through Rafe's thick wavy hair, inviting him in. Her body arched into his exploring hands.

"...a woman like you. It's insane."

His whispered words and disgusted tone penetrated the haze of her wanting. Shame washed over her. Bringing her hands round to his chest, she pushed him away.

"Get off me," she spat at him. "And get out of here. I don't care what Vince asked. I want you gone from here. *Now.*"

"Don't act the enraged virgin with me," Rafe snapped. "A few moments longer and you'd have gone the whole nine yards with me. Don't deny it." He scrubbed the back of his hand across his mouth and wiped it down his shirt-front.

Only too aware he spoke the truth, Trudi didn't wait to hear any more before springing to her feet and running back to the Hall.

I hate him. I hate him.

No matter how many times she repeated the mantra, her body betrayed her. Shame engulfed her. Could he be right? Had she given herself to a stranger the way she'd wanted to a moment ago? Was Rachel the product of nothing more than lust? Given the circumstances of her marriage, she couldn't ignore the possibility. She shivered in the cooling evening air as she rushed headlong back toward the house.

The first thing Trudi remembered after the fateful night eleven years ago was ordering a cup of coffee from a portable roadside café. She remembered the oversized designer silk shirt she wore, tied with a dark tan, quality leather belt. When she'd offered the vendor the twenty-pound note she'd found in the breast pocket, he had become verbally abusive and, filled with fear, she'd grabbed the money and run.

Life, it seemed, repeated itself. Slowing down before reaching the open French doors, Trudi stooped down, rested her hands on her knees and inhaled deeply. If Bella caught sight of her in this state, she'd worry.

Oh my God, what was I thinking to leave the house without ensuring Bella didn't need me?

Hurrying through the study, Trudi quietly entered the den to find Judy reading to Bella. Mouthing a silent "thank you," Trudi backed out and hurried upstairs to her own room. She needed time to get herself together again before she faced anyone else.

❧❦❧

What the hell had happened to him? One moment he'd been trying to get Trudi's wandering attention, the next he'd nearly ravaged her. Rafe didn't like the woman, didn't like the kind of woman she represented. He refused to become another puppet jumping at the end of her string. But God, she'd tasted sweet. And she'd melted in his arms.

For a moment, with those arms wound round his neck, her fingers combing through his hair, her soft breasts pressed against his chest, and the hard buds of her nipples thrusting against him, he'd nearly lost it. Would he have taken her, if she hadn't pushed him away? His thrumming body confirmed the possibility.

Explosive. No other description covered what had happened between them. He may hold her in contempt, but his body had decided it'd found its soul mate.

He knew he'd have to remain out here until the evidence of his wanting disappeared. Shoving his fists into his pockets, he tried to focus on the scene in front of him.

Instead, a pair of flashing amber eyes hid the scene from his gaze. Why did she fascinate him? She stalked his dreams at night and invaded his mind during his waking hours. He'd not enjoyed a moment's peace since his arrival. She represented everything he despised in a woman. Grasping, manipulative, greedy. Always looking to a man to solve her problems, she epitomised everything he reviled in a woman.

She reminded him of the women he sought out for relief back home, and he couldn't understand why didn't he experience the same revulsion with them? Because they didn't expect to find him in their bed the next morning, he told himself.

With a disgusted grunt, Rafe kicked a loose sod of earth across the ground. He didn't want to be in Trudi's bed at night, let alone the following morning. But the memory of her fingers combing through his hair, pulling him closer, had him hard again within seconds. "Damn the woman," he cursed roundly.

Perhaps she had a point. Perhaps he should return to the Hall, phone Arthur and tell him to hell with his request. After all, the place was teaming with retired security personnel, why did Vince and Arthur suppose Rafe's presence would prevent what a bunch of retired qualified field workers couldn't? He'd wanted to discover how much Trudi knew, and now he'd alienated her even more. He'd have to seek her out again to tell her what Vince had discovered about the intruder.

Deciding to give her time to cool down, Rafe sat down again and gazed across the levelled ground ahead.

The choice of site indicated a person sensitive to the needs of others, with an eye for the potential of the surroundings and an appreciation of the peaceful setting for the new tenants.

Rafe remembered Arthur telling him Trudi chose the site, but the man-eating woman he'd seen surely lacked such sensitivity? Had he pegged her wrong? Nah! The memory of her leaping into Arthur's arms on their arrival flashed into his mind.

He pulled an old envelope from his back pocket and began doodling on the back. Half an hour later in the fading light a rough outline for twelve residential chalets covered the creased envelope.

CHAPTER 6

Rafe's distracted gaze settled on the laptop screen in front of him, while images of fawn-like amber eyes invaded his mind. What essence of the woman pulled him in and kept him aching for the touch of her body against his?

Three weeks had passed since that disastrous evening near the chalet site, and he wondered whether he'd ever enjoy a full night's sleep again. Childlike, he knuckled his eyes and pinched the bridge of his nose. He'd seen Trudi do the same thing frequently but hadn't realized until now, he shared the habit.

Or did he? Had he subliminally picked up the practice from her? Huffing in disgust, he tried to re-focus on his laptop. But the image of another pair of amber eyes filled his memory.

ↄ⁀ↄↄ⁀ↄ

Brave, frightened eyes, changing from apprehensive to shocked, then to yearning and awed, and finally to fulfilled and sated. Her dyed-black hair was plastered to her ashen face. He remembered her clothes—her once-white blouse, torn and caked with mud and slime from the river, the remnants of her shredded black skirt clinging to her skinny hips like a bruise.

She looked as if a puff of wind would blow her away, and yet she'd fought like a tigress when her rescuers wanted to admit her to the local hospital. Rafe still remembered how she'd stood in front of him in the hotel room, her chin tilted in bravado, desperate to hide her fear from him.

In spite of the way he'd treated her in order to maintain his role during the poker game, she'd risked her own life to save his. And in exchange? He'd taken advantage of her.

Granted, she'd been willing, but in reality after the trauma she'd been through, she'd probably sought nothing more than comfort and reassurance he'd keep her safe. He'd failed her in the most fundamental way a man could.

They'd come together in a primeval need to celebrate their survival. He acknowledged that but couldn't stop the self-recrimination. His basic sexual urges overruled his inexplicable sense of connection with his saviour. When he woke the following morning, she'd vanished. On the bedside table, next to his wallet, he found his gold pen lying across a single piece of hotel stationery.

IOU—Twenty pounds, one shirt, and a leather belt.

Apart from the remnants of her tattered clothes in the trash bin, she'd left no indication of her presence the night before or where she might have gone while he slept.

After showering and dressing, Rafe called Reception and checked for any messages. Nothing.

He called room service. While he waited for his breakfast to arrive, he phoned his friend, Arthur Clifton. When Arthur failed to pick up, Rafe had wrestled with his conscience.

The woman barely survived the harsh conditions in the water, and she'd become hysterical when someone suggested she go to the hospital to have her injuries seen to. He'd brought her back to his hotel room and helped her into the shower.

Shock from her ordeal robbed her legs of strength, and fully dressed, he walked them both into the shower. Under the hot needles of water, he'd stripped off her bedraggled clothing and soaped and rinsed her torn and battered body. Desire fired his blood and fuelled his need. His clothes joined hers on the bathroom floor. Amazement filled him when he realized her vice-like grip had turned into tremulous strokes down his arms and across his chest. And to his everlasting shame, he'd lost it completely.

Rocked with desire, he wrapped her in one of the large fluffy white towels the hotel provided, scooped her into his arms, and carried her to the bedroom. Laying her on the wide four-poster bed, he'd experienced a fulfilment he'd never known before or since.

The touch of her hands on his body fuelled his desire, and his lips mapped every inch of her. Her moans roared into his blood. Their coupling probably beat the world record, but in his dreams, her scream of fulfilment still rang in his head.

They fell asleep in each other's arms, before waking and sharing another trip to the stars and back. And not uttered one word between them. In retrospect, their union seemed almost sacred to him, an affirmation of survival, a celebration of the future.

When he'd woken to the sunlight drifting through the window, she'd vanished, taking his self-respect with her.

While waiting for Arthur to return his call, he'd sworn never to allow desire to overrule his common sense again. Perhaps it was a gene inherited from his father? Fury, masking self-disgust at his lack of self-discipline, consumed him. If he couldn't control himself around a woman suffering from shock, he obviously couldn't trust himself in any form of permanent relationship in the future.

When Rafe relayed the salient details of the previous night's events, Arthur had been frantic. He'd turned up half an hour later, his face ashen as he paced the floor. He kept asking more and more questions about the woman, demanding information about her whereabouts, and why Rafe had allowed her to slip away. Running his hand through his hair, he continued pacing, firing still more questions. "The bastard told me she'd died in a skiing accident."

"Who?"

"My sister. She believed Cadmore hung the moon and the stars for her, and nothing I said convinced her of his true character. Now, with hindsight, I realize my nagging drove her into his arms. She eloped and married him at one of those instant wedding places in your country. I never saw her again."

"Then this woman is not your sister. Cadmore wagered *his* sister."

In the long silence after Rafe's declaration, Arthur came to an abrupt halt in front of him, his eyes hard and bitter.

"The bastard doesn't have a sister," he snapped and swung away toward the window. "All this time, I believed him." He glanced over his shoulder at Rafe. "He told me she'd died in an avalanche, and they never recovered her body. The bastard lied." Arthur banged his fist into the palm of his other hand then slumped into a wide, soft armchair, his gaze resting sightlessly on Rafe. "He lied. Why would he do that?"

"Are you sure he lied about his sister?"

"I investigated him when Gertrude insisted on seeing him regularly.

∽∾∽

The sound of his laptop going into sleep-mode
disrupted Rafe's thoughts. Automatically he punched a key
and let his thoughts travel back through the years to the
fateful night.

He resurrected images of the first time he'd seen
Cadmore's fake sister.

She reminded him of a long term druggie, with her
lank, shoulder-length, dyed hair, cheap white cotton blouse,
and black skirt. Her scrawny, flat-chested body repulsed
him, and he wondered why Cadmore presumed he'd accept
the woman over his twenty grand. Then Rafe had
wondered why he'd accepted the bet. He'd seen her
unsuccessful attempts to disguise her fear when he'd
handled her like a piece of meat on a butcher's slab during
the card game.

He hadn't gone to the decrepit house to play poker.
He'd gone to learn more about the man who claimed to be
the rightful heir to Lord Kinsale's estates. And to do that,
he'd accepted Cadmore's invitation to join him in an
evening's poker game.

Then he remembered the woman's old scars, small and
round running down her arms, and across her chest
mingled with new bruising from their brush with death.
And the criss-crossed welts on her back, he'd assumed she
received while immersed in the raging river.

But he hadn't told Arthur why Dennis Cadmore lied to him. What good would it do for his friend to learn his sister had become Cadmore's punching bag? If indeed she had been Arthur's sister, and not Cadmore's, as the man had claimed.

Once allowed free reign, the memories kept coming.

₡⁄ᘀ₡⁄ᘀ

"You're wrong, Arthur," Rafe said, trying to re-assure his friend. "You told me your sister is your twin. This woman doesn't look like you at all."

"Fraternal twins, Rafe. Two different eggs conceived at the same time. She's my baby sister by sixteen minutes." Arthur's hands covered his face. "Oh, God! All this time I believed she'd died. Until she met Cadmore, we were close. How come I didn't sense she needed me? I'll never forgive myself." His fingers raked through his hair, and when he looked up, Rafe saw his friend visibly age in front of him.

"You can't be sure, Arthur. And even if you're right, Cadmore may have married again. He said nothing about a wife, and he definitely introduced her as his sister." Rafe crossed to the mini bar and filled two glasses with amber liquid, handing one to Arthur. "Another thing, he called her Rosa. So she's not your sister."

"Gertrude Rosa Clifton. Rosa is her middle name. I've got to find her. Until I do, I'll never be sure."

Arthur's haunted gaze twisted Rafe's gut, and the words of reassurance he wanted to give tumbled away.

How did you find someone, Rafe wondered, who desperately wanted to disappear? Given her circumstances, the woman would make sure no one, especially Dennis Cadmore, would find her. She'd adamantly refused to go to hospital when they'd been rescued from the river. Her fear of Cadmore finding her overrode her need for medical attention. How did Rafe tell Arthur his hopes were doomed?

෴

And now, sitting in front of his laptop in Kinsale Hall eleven years later with the sun slanting in through the narrow window, Rafe had a similar pair of amber eyes haunting his waking hours—

What!

He shot up in his chair as the ghost of a memory chased across his mind. Frantically, he tried to catch it before it slipped away. Impossible!

He stilled his mind and waited.

This woman—Trudi—had old, faded scars on her arms. She'd never worn the skimpy pink tank-top again. Since his arrival, she wore loose, high necked, and long-sleeved shirts. Did that detail bear scrutiny? The line between memories and desire blurred his reality.

The vision of the hussy with her legs wrapped around his friend on his first day seemed alien to the woman he observed now. She exuded an air of inner serenity which soothed everyone who came into contact with her.

Without a word, look, or touch, when in her company, Rafe sensed her calling to him on a level beyond sound or feeling. Beyond the now. Some undefined magnetism drew him toward her, soothing his soul, embalming him with an inner calmness he'd rarely experienced before.

Making him believe in tomorrow.

Frustrating him, when she drew him in like all the other men.

How could he be so wrong? Had his first impressions of the woman he couldn't get out of his mind been so completely mistaken? And why, he asked himself in amazement, had he been so quick to judge her as amoral in the first place? He prided himself in his accurate first impressions of people. His work depended on it.

Early in his career, he'd allowed his ego to dictate a decision, thinking the kudos of designing a house for such a prominent client would go a long way to impressing future ones. The subsequent hassles and constant demands for changes halfway through the building project had taught Rafe a valuable lesson.

Could he be mistaken now?

The woman in charge of Kinsale Hall today was called Delaney. Trudi Delaney.

'*It came to me through my husband.*' Her words clamoured in his brain.

What exactly had she meant?

He needed to talk to Arthur. Pulling his mobile phone from his shirt pocket, he started to dial and then hesitated.

Oh my God! Could the woman in my arms that night really have been Arthur's missing sister?

Shock tore through him, shattering his inner connection and sending his thoughts haywire. Rafe struggled to regain the stillness he needed to let the memories in. Memories he'd avoided for more than a decade.

After a moment's consideration, Rafe dismissed the idea. Arthur's sibling died in a skiing accident.

Then what about the woman Cadmore claimed was his sister? And what really happened to Arthur's twin?

His glance landed on the pile of papers, neatly stacked, beside his laptop. He'd let Rachel and Lizzie use his laptop, and the girls had enjoyed researching Kinsale Hall's history online. He'd turned it into a game for them, encouraging them to discover as much about their home as possible.

He didn't like the thoughts now clamouring for his attention.

In one fluid movement, he shifted from his chair to stand and gaze out of the narrow attic window across the wide expanse of land, bathed in summer sunlight.

He struggled to recall Trudi's words on his arrival. The sunlight created diamonds on the surface of the lake in the wake of the geese floating across the water.

'*I consider myself more in the role of a curator than owner.*'

He tried to recollect the rest of the conversation, something to do with the chalets, but what?

He collected his towel from the adjoining bathroom and headed down the stairs and outside. His long strides brought him to the ideal spot he'd recently found for swimming. Perhaps he'd swim across to the tree-laden island and look around.

Half-an-hour later Rafe lay back on the warm grass. The indignant inhabitants of the island eyed him warily from their perches in the trees, while the ducks and geese peered at him from beneath their wings with false indifference.

'It came to me through my husband.'

Her words barrelled into his head repeatedly. *'It came to me through my husband.'*

The sudden chills running up his spine had nothing to do with the fluffy white clouds blowing across the sun. More words scrolled in front of his inner vision, pinning Rafe where he lay.

Arthur's voice this time. *'Fraternal twins, Rafe. Two different eggs conceived at the same time.'*

With a shake of his head, Rafe dismissed the thoughts again. Trudi's surname was Delaney. If his saviour eleven years ago had been Arthur's sister, her surname would be Cadmore.

Arthur's voice echoed through his head. *'Gertrude Rosa Clifton. Her middle name, Rafe. Rosa is her middle name.'*

And Trudi's comment. *'It came to me through my husband.'* He recognized the intonation of her voice now.

Resignation.

She was tied to the damn place by her sense of duty, like Rafe's birth father before her.

As Rafe refused to be.

He needed to talk to Arthur. And he couldn't risk anyone at the Hall overhearing their conversation. But he needed to talk with his mother first.

ↄↄↄↄↄ

Trudi had managed to avoid Rafe for three weeks, shamefully using the girls by taking them on outings whenever Judy offered to sit with Bella. Or arranging sleepovers for them with their friends, ensuring she ferried them to and from their destinations. On the occasions the girls sought out Rafe's company, Trudi immersed herself in work or spent the time with Bella and Judy. Recently Bella had rallied and enjoyed the warm summer sunshine while gently swinging on the patio lounger.

Trudi's own sketchbook sat neglected on the end of her desk. She hoped to add some more drawings to her growing collection of landscapes. The estate presented endless opportunities to take advantage of the differing light conditions and images. But the continued presence of the trespasser disturbed her sufficiently for her to ensure the girls never strayed far from Kinsale Hall without adult companionship. She missed the safety she normally enjoyed when she wandered from the house in search of a good subject to paint.

Torn between annoyance at Rafe's continued presence at the Hall and relief he seemed happy to let the girls accompany him on his rambles around the estate, Trudi silently acknowledged her gratitude of his approach toward the girls. Now that she'd accepted he was aware of the stranger, she knew regardless of his opinion of her, Rafe wouldn't allow Rachel or Lizzie to come to any harm.

Gathering up her discarded sketchbook, Trudi moved into the den and settled in the chair close to where Bella slept. Sunlight, softened by thin wisps of hazy cloud, fell on the blank page. She began doodling.

Half-an-hour later she studied the image of her nemesis. The bold black pencil lines defined the sculptured high cheek bones, wide brows—a darker shade of honey than his hair—and eyes, which turned from lazy, hazy smoke to gun-metal gray in a blink. She studied the eyes staring back at her from the page. She'd caught an expression she couldn't remember ever seeing in them before.

She wished she understood her feelings for this man. He didn't conceal his contempt for her, and yet he stimulated emotions within her she'd never experienced before. The sight of him shot her pulse rate into the stratosphere. Looking at the image on the page in front of her released a swarm of butterflies in her stomach. And then, there was the anger his presence normally generated.

Even with her twin, Trudi had never experienced the perplexing sense of connection she'd encountered since Rafe's arrival. She'd watched him charm the girls and gain their trust. According to Judy, he often read books and newspapers to Bella. Judy told Trudi Bella had joined her and Rafe in some interesting discussions of his home country and his work.

"He's a good story-teller," Judy said one morning, a few days after Vince had moved Bella down to the den. "And he makes her laugh."

Trudi's fingertip traced the pencil lines on the page. How did the man manage to liquefy her insides with a single look? When had she begun to yearn for a father for the girls, one who'd ruffle their hair the way Rafe did, one who'd manage to fill a room with their laughter simply by telling stories of his niece back home? Why couldn't she forget his touch on her skin and the way his lips crushed hers, hungrily devouring them? Why wasn't she mortified by her desire for more?

Much more.

In turns, she feared the desire consuming her yet was curious about the way she responded to him. It both fascinated and irritated her. How could he do this to her? And what had he done, other than make his derision plain? Why couldn't she understand her attraction to him?

She turned the page and discovered another drawing of Rafe, this time sitting, looking across the chalet site. She'd drawn him from memory, setting him in her recollection, half turned away, his hands clasped round his knees, his hair captured blowing off his forehead.

The inner struggle emanating from her subject leapt from the page. A kind of lost wistfulness.

With a snort of derision, she flipped the page. She'd never met anyone as intransigent as Rafe Hawk. He had his life mapped out. No detours allowed. Well, perhaps the odd one or two, otherwise she wouldn't have to tolerate his presence.

He puzzled her. He didn't want to stay, and yet she sensed some kind of connection. What had Judy said all those weeks ago? Rafe had been roaming through the closed part of the house. Unease whispered down her spine.

Surely not?

Vince wouldn't have asked Rafe to stay if he didn't trust him. But was Rafe's arrival with Arthur shortly after the intruder first turned up simply coincidence? And surely Rafe wouldn't betray such a long-standing friendship with Vince and Arthur?

On the other hand, what did she know of the supposed friendship between the three men?

Perhaps she needed to ditch her pride and contact Vince. She couldn't ask Arthur. According to Bella, he'd introduced Rafe to Vince several years ago. Equally, she couldn't risk ignoring the niggling concern now claiming her attention. She'd have to wait until this evening when the girls went to bed and Rafe had gone up to his room. In the meantime, she'd call Vince's secretary.

"Is he coming back?" Judy moved into the den and looked over Trudi's shoulder at her open sketchbook.

"Who?"

Judy pointed at the sketch of Rafe. "He rang for a taxi this afternoon and took his laptop and bag with him. I wondered whether he'd given you any idea how long he'll be gone."

"I didn't know he'd left." Irritation flooded her. "Where are the girls?"

Why didn't the wretched man have the decency to inform her of his intention to leave?

Did his departure mean the intruder had left?

Careful not to disturb Bella, Trudi plunked her sketchbook on the table and returned to the study with the intention of contacting Vince immediately. She paused, with her hand suspended above the phone as the envelope propped against the lamp caught her attention. Her name written in Rafe's familiar bold writing. Slitting the envelope open, she slipped the sheet of paper out and unfolded it.

Trudi, something has come up, and I'm not sure how long I'll be away. Please keep the girls close to the house. Rafe.

No goodbye or thank you. Between the lines, Trudi read Rafe's unwritten intention to return to Boston without coming back to the Hall. Swiftly, she headed up to his attic room, unsurprised when she discovered the room empty. He'd stripped the bed and placed the used sheets on the chair near the open window. She surveyed the room. Not even the scent of his aftershave remained. Nothing indicated Rafe's intention to return anytime soon. How did the man's presence vanish from a room so quickly? And why did her heart feel as though someone had punched a hole in it?

To hell with waiting to contact Vince. Trudi raced down the narrow stairs along the landing and down the main staircase and came to a skidding halt in front of a stranger standing in the open doorway.

"I'm sorry, can I help you?" Trudi asked. She'd never seen her before, but something vaguely familiar about the woman nagged at her.

Thick shoulder length brown hair framed her slender face and neck. Her loose fitting olive green silk shirt topped burnt-orange fitted pants. Petite. Trudi couldn't find another word to describe the elegant woman standing in front of her.

"I'm looking for Rafe Hawk."

"Oh. I'm sorry. He's not here."

"I've come straight from the airport. If you don't mind, I'll wait for him to return."

Dismayed, Trudi spotted the pile of luggage sitting in the doorway then turned to study the other woman more closely. Dark smudges beneath her eyes testified to her weariness. Stepping forward, Trudi clasped the woman's hand and drew her gently into the study. "First let me get you a cup of coffee or tea," she offered as she led the stranger to the only armchair left in the room. "I'm Trudi."

"Thank you. I'm Megan. Megan Cantral. When will Rafe be back?"

For the first time, Trudi noticed her American accent. "I'm afraid you've just missed him. And he didn't say when he'd be back." She watched the stranger slump back in her chair. "If there's anything I can do to help—?"

"I let the taxi go. Please will you tell me where I can find Rafe?" Tears filled the woman's eyes. Trudi watched her will them away.

"He didn't say. I discovered he'd left a short while ago, but I can make some enquiries. In the meantime, I suggest you let us put you up overnight. We have plenty of room." Trudi smiled down at the woman. "And I'll arrange for you to join him tomorrow, when I've discovered his destination."

Swallowing a sigh of frustration, Trudi decided her call to Vince would have to wait a few moments longer. Or would it? Perhaps he'd know where Rafe had gone and why he'd left in such a hurry.

Settling the newcomer with her cup of tea and some biscuits, Trudi excused herself and returned upstairs to use the phone in her bedroom. Vince wasn't there, but Heather assured Trudi she'd page her boss and ask him to return the call.

Before returning to the study, Trudi needed to get her thoughts together. Rafe's sudden departure left her feeling vulnerable and exposed. But to what, she wasn't sure.

Had Rafe discovered the trespasser's identity and decided to leave? Were he and the intruder connected in some way? Why hadn't he bothered to tell anyone about his decision to leave? What caused Rafe's all-fired hurry to go? And why the heck did she care? Why did his sudden absence leave her feeling she'd lost some integral part of herself?

Was the woman downstairs Rafe's girlfriend?

If so, why had Rafe kissed her the way he did that night at the chalet site?

With a start of dismay, Trudi realized that for all the time Rafe spent with them, she'd learned very little about the man, other than his impact on her emotions. One kiss and she'd been ready to jump his bones.

Physical attraction. Nothing more. And she'd never act on it. With a huff of self-disgust at her dithering, Trudi headed back down to the study.

A stranger walking in on Judy and Megan might assume they'd known each other for a lifetime. Reaching the doorway, Trudi heard Megan mention someone called Tammy, and instantly the memory of Rafe mentioning his niece soon after his arrival came to mind. Did that make Megan a member of Rafe's family, if they both knew Tammy?

"I'm sorry to leave you like that." Trudi poured some lukewarm tea from the pot and carried it across to her desk before settling in the chair behind it.

"Have you discovered where Rafe's gone?" Megan asked. "When he emailed me yesterday, I got the impression he'd intended to stay here for a while longer."

"If he knew you intended to visit him, I'm surprised he didn't let you know his change of plans." Trudi smiled across her desk.

"Oh, he wasn't expecting me. I made a spur of the moment decision. I need his advice on something."

Trudi noticed tears fill Megan's eyes. "I can't get hold of the person who might tell me where Rafe has gone, but his secretary has promised to ask him to contact me when he gets her message. In the meantime, let me show you to your room."

A quick glance in the direction of the den, reassured Trudi the girls were happily entertaining Bella.

"Don't worry about your luggage. It'll be safe on the steps, and I'll bring it up to you shortly. Perhaps you'd like to rest after your flight?" Trudi lead the way upstairs and opened the door for Megan to enter the room opposite her own. "I hope you'll be comfortable here. There's an en-suite bath, and I'll bring you your own tea and coffee makers. If there's anything else you need, please don't hesitate to ask."

Quietly, Trudi closed the door behind her and left Megan to settle in. She wondered what had upset the woman so much she'd flown to England to visit Rafe without telling him first.

CHAPTER 7

The sound of Vince's pager replaced the fading noise of the plane disappearing into the clouds. Moving swiftly through the crowds, he found a quiet spot and speed dialled his secretary. When Arthur discovered Rafe had left for Boston, he'd have a great deal to say and none of it complimentary.

"Heather?"

"Where have you been? I've been calling you for ages. Trudi rang about an hour ago and wants you to call her back ASAP."

"Right, I'll get on to it. Did she say why?"

Heather chuckled. "No, but she's mad about something."

"No kidding, and I can guess what she's mad about too," he added with a chuckle of his own.

"What's going on, Vince." No trace of laughter remained. "She never calls without reason, and she didn't mentioned Bella, so something else, equally important, must have happened."

"Don't worry. I'll contact her as soon as I get out of here."

"Where are you?"

"The airport."

"What's going on? She repeated. "Has there been another terrorist alert?"

"No, nothing like that. I've seen a friend off on his flight home." Vince grinned, anticipating Arthur's reaction when he discovered all his plans had gone awry. "I'll see you tomorrow." He snapped his mobile phone closed and strode to his waiting car.

Once on the motorway, he gave way to his thoughts. Arthur was playing a dangerous game, one that might hurt his sister badly. And Rachel, too. He'd wondered what had drawn Bella's attention when he'd seen her studying Rafe the day he arrived at the Hall. Then Vince had understood.

After that, it hadn't taken him long to recognize Arthur's hand behind efforts to get Rafe to remain at the Hall. Arthur's request for Vince to ensure Rafe stayed to watch out for the intruder and to protect Trudi, Bella, the girls, and a houseful of agents confirmed his suspicions, and left him wary of the consequences.

Now Rafe was putting the pieces together for himself, and he wasn't too happy. Did Trudi's phone call have anything to do with Rafe's sudden departure? He pressed the speed dial and waited.

Why hadn't Trudi said anything about the trespasser? If Judy hadn't told him, how long would Trudi have kept silent? The more he considered it the more his irritation intensified. Her lack of action put them all in danger. Surely she recognized that?

How could she? a small voice in his head asked. *You didn't tell her Bella's ex left prison recently.*

"Shit!" He thumped his fist on the steering wheel. With Rafe gone, he'd be forced to tell Trudi, to ensure she kept the girls close, but without confiding in her fully.

Rafe's garbled half-speculations would not remain contained in Boston much longer. Experience had taught Vince that information gathered a momentum of its own, once released. Apparently, unrelated incidents fell into place. Soon everyone involved would recognize the whole picture. Trudi would be devastated, possibly destroyed. And that would have a knock-out effect on Bella and the girls. "Shit, shit, shit!"

The sudden crackle of his phone alerted Vince. "Arthur?"

"What's up? Where are you?"

"I'm on the motorway, heading for the Hall. And I suggest you get your butt over there ASAP."

"What's going on? Has the intruder made a move yet?" Arthur refrained from mentioning names over the phone.

They'd identified the trespasser soon after his arrival in the area.

"That's not the problem right now, but something will go down soon."

"Why? What's happened to bring things to a head? We didn't anticipate any movement before—"

"Rafe's gone," Vince snapped, annoyed again by Arthur's ill-advised manipulations.

"Gone?" Arthur's astonished voice filled the car. "What do you mean, gone? Where?"

"I've seen him off on a plane for Boston, and he's not too pleased with you."

Vince noted Arthur's hesitation before he spoke. "Why on earth would Rafe be mad at me?"

"Stop messing me about! No one likes being played for a sucker," Vince snapped. "In your haste to play puppeteer, did you once stop to weigh up the consequences your actions might have on your sister and niece? Not to mention Bella and Lizzie? How could you do it?"

"What exactly are you implying?" Arthur's cold tones vibrated across the ether.

"I'm not *implying* anything. Don't play me for a fool. I supported your efforts to ensure Trudi inherited the Hall after Dennis Cadmore's death," Vince said. "We spent months trying to trace her when Rafe escaped from Cadmore's house, all those years ago, with the supposed sister. Did you really think I couldn't work out the connection? I do wonder why you took so long to make your move."

"If you knew so damn much, why didn't you mention it before now?" Arthur demanded.

"If you'd been straight with me from the start, we may have found Trudi instead of waiting for someone to stumble across her identity. Fortunately for us, and quite by chance, may I remind you, Serena made the connection."

The countryside slipped past the car, and soon Vince turned off the motorway to follow the rural road to the Hall. "Heather said Trudi's mad, so if you're not on your way, I suggest you get your butt off whatever chair it's in and move it."

Vince changed gears and swung the car through the large metal gates leading to the Hall. Why would Rafe's departure anger Trudi? According to Judy they avoided each other whenever possible. He could understand her anger when Rafe left without telling anyone, but he knew Trudi rarely lost her cool. No. Some more disturbing reason accounted for Trudi's rage.

Pulling up in front of the massive studded wooden front doors, he leaned forward, angled his head to glance through the windshield, and stared.

He'd never seen such a beautiful woman before. She stood on the porch, her trim figure dressed in shirt and slacks, her brown hair resting on her shoulders. Something deep within him shifted.

He wasn't aware of leaving the car or reaching the top steps. His mind was focussed on her delicate fingers now resting in his hand.

"I didn't realize Trudi had visitors," he said.

Her smile reminded him of the sun coming out from behind a bank of dark rain clouds, while another part of his brain cringed at the metaphor. "Strictly speaking, I'm not."

Vince recognized her American accent. "Then perhaps I'm correct in assuming you've come to visit Rafe?"

Surprise widened her gray-green eyes. "How did you know?"

"Your accent."

"Oh." Her smile faded. "I wanted to talk to Rafe, but I gather he left shortly before I got here. It seems no one knows where he is."

"I'm afraid he's gone back to Boston."

The woman's shoulders drooped. "Why would he do that? I emailed him last night, and he never mentioned anything about going home. I don't understand. Did he say why he's gone home?"

"He didn't confide in me, I'm afraid. He's knows my friend Arthur better. I'm Vince Parker, by the way. I met Rafe several years ago. On this occasion, I visited my sister the day Rafe arrived here with Arthur." He put his hand carefully on the small of the woman's back and guided her into the main hall.

"I'm Megan Cantral, Rafe's sister."

"I'm pleased to meet you, Megan, and I'm sorry you missed your brother. I hope you'll agree to stay until we can contact him. In the meantime, if I can do anything to help, please don't hesitate to ask."

He wanted to fold her into his arms and cover her soft delicate pink lips with his. He wanted…

What did he want? He'd never before met a woman who instantly fired his blood. He wasn't a hearth and slippers man, but he'd happily see her slippers in front of his hearth for the long haul. The sudden craziness unsettled him.

"Vince." Trudi's sharp tone startled him out of his fantasy.

"Trudi. Heather said you called."

Her fury slapped at him. "What's brought you down here?"

"And it's nice to see you, too."

With a twist of her lips and a twinkle in her eye, Trudi moved forward to place a carefully aimed peck on his cheek. "I expected a return call, not for you to come tearing over without finding out what I wanted."

"Would you like me to leave, ring you, and return again?" Vince couldn't hold back a smile.

With a punch on his chest Trudi headed for the study. "Tell us why you've come this afternoon. Oh, and by the way, what's happened to the scumbag you dumped on me?"

Oops, apparently Megan Cantral hadn't revealed her full identity to Trudi. How would Trudi react when she found out? Vince took a step back.

Before he uttered a word, she continued. "The louse left without a word to anyone. How come he suddenly decides to up sticks and walk out like this, when previously you swore lives depended on his presence here? I told you he didn't want to remain here anymore than I wanted him here, and that's saying something. And—" she stabbed the air in front of his face with her finger. "The intruder's still here. I saw him moments before you arrived. Although for a bit there, I wondered whether the he and Rafe were in league with each other," Trudi added belligerently.

"Oh yes," Vince breathed. "The trespasser. The one you happened not to mention. And why, do you suppose, did you neglect to pass on that small, but possibly significant piece of information?"

"Vince, don't play the heavy-handed brother figure with me. It could have been a farm hand or anyone."

"Anyone, Trudi?" Vince snapped, unable to contain his mounting anger.

ೕംೕം

"Why should you think my brother was in league with someone?" Megan's perplexed voice interrupted Vince's tirade.

Shock drained the color out of Trudi's face. Her gaze shifted from Vince to the newcomer. "Brother? Are you saying the person watching this house for the past several weeks is your brother?"

"What are you talking about? Why would Rafe want to watch this place?" Bewildered, Megan faced Trudi. "He told me Arthur and Vince asked him to remain for a short while."

"You're Rafe's sister?" Trudi swiped her brow with the back of her hand, struggling to make sense of Megan's revelation. Why would Rafe leave if he expected his sister to visit?

Answer: he hadn't expected her. So why had she turned up out of the blue like this? Before she followed through on her thoughts, the sound of another car pulling up outside had Trudi moving back into the hallway. The others followed her.

"Arthur?" She turned toward Vince. "What's going on? Why are you both here when Rafe's left?" Seriously worried now and trying to conceal it, she watched her brother run up the steps and join them.

Unable to interpret the glances winging between the men, Trudi swung round at the sound of her daughter's voice coming from the study doorway.

"…is that Okay?" Rachel barrelled into the hall and hugged her mother round her waist.

"Tammy?" Megan stared at Rachel as though she'd seen a ghost.

"Back up, hon. Is what alright?" Vaguely aware of the commotion behind her, Trudi hunkered down to kiss her daughter's cheek.

"Who is she?" Rachel asked, gazing over Trudi's shoulder in alarm. "And why has she fainted?"

A swift glance at the scene told Trudi the men had the situation in hand, even if she was more confused by the second.

"What the devil——?" Arthur rushed forward to catch the collapsing woman before she hit the ground, but Vince reached her first.

Swiftly, Trudi turned back to Rachel. "What did you want? Tell me quickly, I have to help Megan."

"Bella wants to sit outside." Rachel shifted from one foot to the other, obviously shaken by the sight of a complete stranger collapsing in front of her like that.

Anger and fear fingered up Trudi's spine. Her intuition screamed warnings in her brain, linking all the individual events of the afternoon. But right now she didn't have time to try and connect the dots.

"Arthur? I mean to get to the bottom of what's going on, and why you and Vince have both turned up out of the blue like this. In the meantime please go and help Bella while I deal with this situation."

She cast a reassuring smile at Rachel. "Sweetheart, go with your uncle, and I'll join you in a few minutes." Trudi watched her daughter return to the den before focussing on the scene behind her.

With a deep sigh and a sense of impending doom, she turned to discover Vince cradling Megan's head in his lap and gently stroking her hair away from her face. Amongst the uproar, Trudi registered her amazement at Vince's tender actions. Shaking her head to clear it, she bent down and clasped Megan's shoulders, pulling her carefully forward before pushing her head between her knees.

"What's going on here Vince?" Trudi asked. "And don't fob me off. Before this day's over, you and I are going to have a long talk. In the meantime, perhaps you will bring Megan through to the study. She's coming round."

Her spine straight and her chin high, Trudi stalked into the study and switched on her electric kettle. A hot sweet drink would help Megan, who'd obviously suffered some kind of shock. But Trudi couldn't begin to guess why.

❧❧❧

"Rafe, I'm glad you're home. First Tammy disappeared, and now Megan has." Martha Hawk flew into her son's arms.

"Mother?" Rafe dropped his bags and laptop on the floor and wrapped his arms round her distraught figure. "What do you mean they've disappeared? Everything seemed okay last night when Megan emailed me. What's happened?" Swiftly, he tried to adjust the time difference between Kinsale Hall and his sister's home. "Megan told me Tammy went over to Cheryl's for a sleepover they arranged last week. Have you been in touch with them?"

"Of course we have." his mother huffed. "How do you suppose we discovered she's missing? Cheryl's Mom rang to ask why Tammy hadn't arrived. They'd expected her three hours earlier but didn't contact us before because they assumed she'd been delayed. When she tried to contact Megan and she didn't answer, they rang here."

"Have you contacted the police?" He urged his mother into her usual chair and moved across the room to the wet-bar.

"Of course we have," she repeated. "They believe they've gone off somewhere together without telling anyone."

"Why on earth would they believe that?" Rafe shoved a glass of brandy into his mother's hand before tossing back the amber liquid in his own and swallowing the contents in one gulp. He wished he could hop onto a flight to New York and make more enquiries himself. He tried to mask his panic and stay calm in front of his mother. "Start at the beginning and tell me what happened."

"The police refuse to take action until they hear from Megan." His mother took another sip of brandy. "I'm not sure of the details. Megan rang me last night for advice. Apparently, she and Tammy had an argument about Matthew."

"Matthew? What does he have to do with anything? He died four years ago. Megan told me she answered any questions Tammy asked about her Dad. Why would they fall out about him now?" Genuinely puzzled, Rafe sat beside his mother and gently wrapped his hand round her free one.

They were a close and happy family and totally devastated when Matthew died in a hit-and-run accident. Unusually, the police caught the driver, who'd been convicted and jailed. Rafe thought his sister and niece had come to terms with their loss. Apparently, he'd been wrong there, too.

"It seems Tammy arranged to go over to Cheryl's house after lunch. Megan offered to drive her, but Tammy had refused to speak to her mother since she got up. She simply walked out the door. I suppose Meg assumed she'd gone straight to Cheryl's.

"When Tammy hadn't arrived three hours after they expected her, Cheryl's mother tried to reach Megan. After an hour, she rang me. In the meantime, Cheryl and her parents had searched the streets between the two houses, knocking on doors asking whether anyone had seen Tammy walking past.

"And when they still couldn't contact Megan, they phoned the police. But they refused to act. They insisted mother and daughter had probably gone off somewhere together. They said if her family was concerned, they should file a missing person's report.

"Cheryl's Mom contacted me and told me what the police said. Of course, I filed a report, and we kept trying to phone Megan. But she's not answering at home, and her cell is switched off. Luke flew out. The place is empty, and he's agreed to stay in case Tammy, and or, Megan come home."

"When did Tammy go missing?"

"Over twenty-four hours ago." Tears spilled down his mother's cheeks.

"Has any note or demand of any kind been received or found?"

"No."

Fear ripped through Rafe. What was so terrible about the argument between Tammy and her mother she'd stay away for over twenty-four hours? Unless—

He didn't even want to go there. And what about Megan? Why leave the house unattended? What if someone abducted Tammy and tried to make contact?

Gut wrenching dread engulfed him. Rafe filled his glass again.

After a delayed take-off followed by a holding pattern before landing, he'd come straight from the airport intending to discuss his suspicions about events back in England. And now this. Wearily, he rubbed the back of his neck before pinching the bridge of his nose between his thumb and finger. The ring-tone of his cell phone shattered the silence in the comfortable living room.

"Yes," he snapped, paused to listen before exploding. "Where the hell are you?" He glanced at his mother and silently mouthed his sister's name. "You're where? What the hell possessed you to go there?" He lowered the phone from his ear. "She flew to England to talk to me. The silly bitch flew to England."

"Don't' call me a silly bitch." His sister's voice screeched across the airwaves. "You wait until you have a daughter of your own, then you'll understand."

If only she knew! Rafe's thoughts crashed around him. If his suspicions were correct, his own daughter was the same age as Tammy, and living on the estate he'd adamantly refused to have anything to do with over a decade ago.

crocro

"Rafe! Rafe, are you still there? I'm at the Hall with your sister."

Vince's brisk tones steadied Rafe's struggle to marshal the emotions battering him. "Vince? What the hell is Megan doing there? Is her daughter, Tammy, with her?" Rafe could hear footsteps at the other end of the phone. "What the hell's going on?"

"A few moments ago Megan spotted Rachel and mistook her for Tammy. I don't need to tell you how shocked Megan is right now. This whole thing has blown wide open. And my first concern is for Trudi and Rachel. I think you'd better get back here as soon as you can."

"I can't. Tammy's missing. When Megan didn't answer her phone, we filed a missing person's report on both of them. My brother flew out to her place and stayed in case Tammy rang home."

"I'll log a flight plan and bring Megan back. Do you need to know anything else from Megan?"

"Yes, you better put her back on so we can focus our search for Tammy." Even as he spoke, an idea curled into his mind, but he dismissed it.

Tammy had been her Daddy's princess. They'd done everything together, and his death had devastated the six-year-old child. For months she'd asked everyone she met, whether they'd seen her Daddy. Now, four years on would she visit his graveside alone? And where had she gone since?

Rachel's image floated in front of his eyes. If anything happened to her, he couldn't imagine how he'd feel. He didn't even know whether his suspicions were justified. And if they were, how would Trudi react? Why hadn't she said anything to him? He'd known her long enough to be fairly certain she couldn't maintain a deliberate deception during those weeks without slipping up. So what were the missing pieces of the puzzle? How could he spend all that time with Rachel and not recognize her?

When he'd posed that question at the airport, Vince had declined to speculate. He'd insisted Rafe talk to Arthur.

Vince had tried to persuade him to stay, but consumed by confusion and rage, Rafe insisted he needed time to reflect on events. If he'd waited for Arthur, he might have smashed the guy's face in if he verified Rafe's suspicions.

Rafe could hear Vince's muted tones on the phone ad he waited for Megan.

"Rafe? I'm sorry but Tammy and I had a fight—"

"I know. What about?"

"You don't understand. She's here. I've just seen her. She told me she was going to come and live with you. And she's here, safe."

The emotion in his sister's voice almost destroyed him, and Rafe wished he didn't have to shatter her dreams. He remembered his own surprise when he'd first seen Rachel, and her similarity to Tammy, without questioning his reactions further. Why should he? Lots of unrelated folks resembled one another. Didn't they say everyone had at least one doppelganger?

"Megan, honey, she's not Tammy. Rachel is Trudi's daughter." And mine, he wanted to add, but remained silent.

"No, you're wrong. I've seen her. I tell you, it's Tammy. I have to find out how and why she got here. But she's safe."

Trudi's bewildered voice in the background filtered between Megan's protests. Fool! If only he'd stayed, he would be there for Trudi and Rachel. Instead thousands of miles separated them, and he'd committed to searching for his niece.

"Meggie, Vince will bring you home. We need you here. You can trust him. I want you to come straight back home with him now."

"What's going on?"

He heard a rustling at the other end of the phone, and then Vince's voice reached him. "I'll bring her home. Leave her with me, and do what you can at your end." Vince cut off the call, and Rafe turned to see his mother watching him.

"Who is Rachel?"

How did mothers do that? How could they zero in on the one subject in a conversation you least wanted them to? "I promise I'll tell you later, but right now, it seems Megan flew to England because Tammy told her she was going to come and live with me."

"Oh." His mother jumped up her eyes alight with excitement.

"She isn't there, Mom." Rafe hated to dim his mother's anticipation and was surprised when it didn't happen.

"No, but perhaps she's at your apartment. Would the commissionaire let her in if she arrived there?"

"Yes, they would." Rafe admitted after a short consideration. "Both Rex and Jason know her and would let her come right on up before checking with me."

"Come on then, let's not waste any more time. Let's go and see."

"Wait a minute, Mom. We have to think. How's she going to get to my apartment from home? Did she have enough money with her? We can forget the airports. They're not going to allow a ten-year-old on a plane without adult supervision. So unless she stowed away, we can forget them," he repeated.

"That leaves the Greyhound/Peter Pan busses, or hitching. God forbid she'd attempt to hitch. Yeah! I better phone my apartment. If she doesn't answer then we have to try and decide what actions she'd take and try to recreate them so we can trace her." He took his mother's mangled hankie out of her fretting fingers and dried her tears with it.

"Give me a moment to ring first before we head over to my apartment. If she's not there we'll use it as a base for extending our search." Rafe hugged his mother briefly and pulled out his cell phone.

CHAPTER 8

"I'm not leaving without my daughter." Megan rushed past Vince toward the den. "I'm not leaving without her."

Trudi stepped forward and wrapped her arms around the distraught woman to prevent Megan from disturbing Bella any further.

"Rachel is my daughter," she said, trying to calm Rafe's sister.

"Liar! Liar!" Megan screamed, pushing Trudi aside. "I know when I've seen my daughter. You've got my Tammy, and I'm not leaving alone."

"She isn't Tammy, Megan." Vince stepped in front of the now hysterical woman. "You only have to hear her speak to realize she's not your daughter."

"Why would you say such terrible things to me?" Megan didn't believe him. "Look at her photograph. That child is my daughter Tammy." Scrabbling for the bag on the floor, Megan pulled out a postcard-sized photograph and passed it to Vince.

At a sound from the doorway, Megan looked beyond Vince at the terrified face of her daughter's look-alike studying the emotional group in the middle of the study.

"You're not my mother. And if you treat your daughter like you're treating my family, I don't blame her for not wanting to stay with you anymore." Rachel's fear-induced anger evaporated in a hic-cup.

The child's distinctly English accent denied her American parentage, and fresh tears streamed down Megan's face.

"Rachel!" Trudi gasped in dismay. "Apologize for your rudeness immediately."

"I won't. She said horrid things about us. She said you stole her daughter. She's the one who should apologize." Rachel swung on her heel and stormed back into the den, remembering in time to close the door quietly behind her.

"I'm sorry." Megan moved away from the warmth of Vince's supportive embrace and passed the photograph across for Trudi to examine. "They might be twins."

Trudi studied the picture of a child so similar to Rachel, she agreed the two girls could indeed be mistaken for twins. She felt the blood drain from her face. Sparks of blinding white light flashed behind her eyes. A stabbing pain forced her to her knees.

She recognized understanding in Vince's eyes, when he dropped down beside her.

"You know what's going on here, don't you?" she asked.

The truth written in his face rocked her back on her heels. With an awful sense of clarity, the missing links snapped into place. The pounding inside her skull increased.

"You knew!" Terror ripped through her. She fought against the white light bursting across the back of her eyes and tried to maintain a grip on her concentration. "You knew about this." Waving the photograph in front of his face, Trudi tried to control her voice. "You bastard. You knew his identity and still invited him to stay."

Fear and betrayal jostled for supremacy. "Get out. Get out of here and take her with you." Trudi pointed a trembling finger toward Megan's shocked face.

Realizing Rafe had come here knowing he had a daughter sent terror coursing through Trudi's veins. But if so, why had he left so suddenly? And what did he intend to do about Rachel now? Nothing and no one would take Rachel away. Anyone who tried would regret the attempt, Trudi promised herself.

"I suspected. When I spoke to Rafe earlier at the airport." Vince bent down and reached out to lay a comforting hand on her shoulder. "It was no more than conjecture."

"Don't touch me." Trudi twisted out of his reach. "I don't believe you. I thought you were a friend. I trusted you, you bastard. Don't ever come near me again."

"Bella—"

"What about Bella, Vince?" Wrapped in an alien sense of detachment, Trudi watched him reel back at the venom in her voice. "You used both of us for your own ends. Be sure you stay out of my way in future when you visit her again. Now get out and take her with you." Trudi waved her hand in Megan's direction. "And you," pulling her shoulders back, and lifting her chin, Trudi stood and faced Megan. "You can tell your brother from me, if he tries to take my daughter away from me, I'll charge him with rape."

"Mummy?" Rachel's hesitant voice dropped into the shocked silence.

With an indrawn breath Trudi pulled herself together and turned a false smile toward her daughter. "Yes, hon?" Swiftly she reached out and swept Rachel into her arms, ignoring the other two occupants of the room.

"Bella wants Vince to explain what everyone's shouting about."

"Vince." Trudi turned to him with a warning glance, before nodding toward the den. She may never want to set eyes on Bella's conniving brother again, but she wouldn't dream of keeping the siblings apart.

The stench of her fear filled her nostrils, settled in the pit of her stomach, and threatened to choke her. Trudi pinched the bridge of her nose in an effort to stave off the blackness threatening to engulf her. She looked up in time to see the dawning horror reflecting Megan's eyes. The sudden pressure of trying to regain forgotten memories increased the pounding in her head, and the heaviness behind her eyes threatened to explode. Everything in the room shimmered and merged.

"What's going on?" Arthur burst into the room, closely followed by Judy. "We heard you from outside by the car." His glance took in the frozen tableau in front of him.

"She," Rachel pointed toward Megan, "called Mummy a liar. She said I was someone called Tammy, and she was going to take me back to America with her. I won't go." Tears flowed down the frightened child's face. "And she can't make me."

"Don't be silly, Rachel. No one is going to take you anywhere." Arthur snapped, before turning on the newcomer. "Whatever possessed you to make such a daft accusation?"

Wordlessly Trudi held out the photograph Megan had given Vince.

"What is—? I'm sorry I don't know your name." Arthur turned to Megan.

"Megan Cantral," She replied. "I'm Rafe's sister."

"What are you doing with a photograph of Rachel?" He looked more closely at the picture. "I have to say it's a good one, but I don't recognize the background."

"Because that's my daughter Tammy, and I took the picture in New York, earlier this year." Megan said woodenly.

Overwhelmed, Trudi viewed the events unfolding before her with a strange sense of detachment.

"I suggest before anyone goes anywhere, we try and discover what caused this mistaken identity." Judy turned to the sideboard and poured a large scotch into a tumbler before pressing it into Megan's hand. "Drink this, it will help."

Judy took the photograph from Trudi's nerveless fingers, pursing her lips in silent understanding before turning to study Megan. "Why did you expect to find your daughter here?"

"Tammy arranged to sleep over with her friend, and I offered to take her, but we'd fallen out over something so trivial I can't even remember what now. Children say and do things they don't mean when they're upset, and I didn't expect her to try and find her uncle. When I emailed Rafe yesterday, he never mentioned anything about returning to Boston. It seemed an ideal chance to come over here and talk to him about Tam and our argument. When I saw your little girl—" She looked at Trudi. "I mistook her for Tammy."

Trudi forced herself up off her knees and forward. She reached for Megan's hand. "I understand what happened is upsetting. But why don't you ring Tammy's friend and speak to her? I'm sure you'll both feel better once you've talked things through."

"Why should you care? After what I said to you, you should be pushing me out the door."

"Believe me, I want to." The travesty of a smile didn't reach Trudi's eyes, but the other woman's pain began to touch her shattered emotions. "It won't solve anything.

"If you tell us why you expected your daughter to be here, I'm sure, if Arthur and Vince apply their minds, they will come up with something. It may even be something useful. You never know your luck," Trudi added cynically as Judy's snort of laughter turned into a strategic fit of coughing.

"I didn't expect to see her here, that's why seeing your daughter was a shock. Everything went clean out of my mind. Tammy is sleeping over with her friend. If you'll excuse me, I need to talk with her."

A few moments later, they stared in horror at a white lipped Megan. "She's not there. She never arrived, and everyone is out searching for her. I have to return home." Frantically Megan began dialling again and obviously realized she didn't have the number for the airport. "I need to arrange a flight to Boston."

"Boston?" Arthur queried. "You said you lived in New York?"

"We do, but Tammy told me before she left she would go and stay with Rafe. They said she may be trying to get to Boston from New York."

An appalled silence filled the room as everyone visualised a ten year old striking out on her own on such a journey.

"Mummy," Rachel's trembling voice penetrated Trudi's attention. "Mummy, you won't let her take me away, will you?"

"No sweetheart I won't ever let *anyone* take you away." Trudi held Megan's gaze squarely, until the other woman lowered her eyes. "Megan's upset because you reminded her of her daughter, Tammy. Now your Uncles Vince and Arthur are going to help her find her."

"Trudi—" Arthur reached out to take her arm.

"Stay away from me Arthur." Trudi turned on him, her eyes flashing. "So help me, if you come near me right now, I won't be responsible for my actions. You've deceived me and used me for you own reasons. And if you think I'm about to forgive you right now, you're badly mistaken."

Arthur reeled back as if she'd hit him. "Trudi, you can't mean that."

"Believe me, I mean it. And if I find myself embroiled in a custody battle because of your interference, I swear I'll never speak to you again." Trudi brushed her lips against the softness of Rachel's hair and headed for the den.

"I can do nothing more here, so I'm going to sit with Bella," she snapped over her shoulder. "I suggest you and Vince apply yourselves to something constructive like helping Megan find her daughter." She swept out of the room with Rachel, leaving a stunned silence behind.

Staggering from the similarities of Rachel and the child in the photograph, Trudi tried to come to terms with the thoughts hammering against her skull. Did the vague memory of an American accent hovering in her mind represent lost memories? Or imaginings she desperately wanted to be true? Did the vague skittering of unease the day Rafe had arrived signify some kind of subliminal recognition on her part? And what of the future?

"Why did that lady say she would take me away with her?"

Rachel's frightened query recalled Trudi back to the present. It couldn't be true. It was a mistake, a bad dream, a coincidence Rafe's niece and her daughter looked so similar.

"When she saw you, she mistook you for her own little girl and thought her daughter had come to visit her Uncle Rafe." Trudi could almost sympathize with the other woman's shock.

What would happen if the child in the photograph turned out to be Rachel's blood relation? Trudi wished she remembered the circumstances of her daughter's conception.

If it were true, Trudi wondered how Rafe's family would react when they learned about it. How would Megan explain the discovery to them? Or had Rafe already said something to his family? Would he try to claim Rachel, using the power of his family to take her daughter away from her?

Until this moment she'd never expected Rachel's father to figure in their lives. He'd have rights of access, she supposed. Raw fear threatened to engulf her.

She remembered escaping from her husband's house with someone.

But no matter how she'd tried, none of her efforts revealed the face of her companion that night.

Months later, when the doctors discovered Trudi didn't remember the father of her child, careful questioning by the medical staff led her doctor to believe she'd lost roughly one to seven days from her memory.

Surely that meant...What did it mean?

Too tired and emotionally drained to work out anything else, she blanked her mind to her roiling thoughts.

Arthur and Vince's duplicity stunned her. She doubted she'd ever trust them again. The sensation of dancing to the manipulative strings held by unknown hands sent a shaft of anger coursing through her.

Several moments passed before she regained control of her emotions.

But by the time she joined Bella, apart from the faint trail of tears on her pale cheeks nothing of the recent turmoil showed on her face.

ↄↄↄ

"I'm sorry," Megan whispered. "I'm so sorry. I should never have come here. I've caused nothing but grief. I mean, I didn't stop to think. I was scared. All I could hear was Tammy telling me she wanted to live with Rafe because he loved her, and I didn't. I wanted to talk it out with him. Since Matthew died, Tammy has turned to her uncle more and more." Fresh tears streamed down Megan's face.

"I don't understand." At Arthur's troubled expression, Megan added, "The little girl? Rachel? Rafe's never said anything at home about having a daughter. And he wouldn't deny the existence of his child if he knew about it. They are so alike, surely they're related?"

"It's complicated, and not my place to speculate," Arthur said. "But something Vince said to me before I got here, leads me to believe Rafe may have begun to consider the possibility."

Still shocked from the scene he'd witnessed and his sister's fury, Arthur placed a reassuring hand on the frightened woman's shoulder.

He'd never seen his sister so angry before. With every passing second, he felt the chasm growing between them. When she'd whipped round and faced him with her barrage of accusations, he wondered whether they'd ever manage to bridge it again.

He tried tuning into the natural connection linking twins and sensed a dead emptiness. And he didn't know what to do. For this to happen after everything she'd been through. A pain, akin to a knife in his chest, tore through him at the prospect of Trudi never speaking to him again.

He knew his twin. Slow to anger, but when someone hurt her as deeply as she hurt right now, she would hesitate to trust them again. He'd just have to wait and hope.

The strident sound of the phone on Trudi's desk startled them. Vince returned to the study, swiftly crossed the room, and lifted the receiver.

With two distraught women on his hands, Arthur wondered which needed Judy's support the most. In the end he decided in favor of the Megan. His sister wouldn't thank him for what she'd consider his interference.

"Yes?"

In response to Vince's slight inclination of his head, Arthur moved closer to the desk.

"Yes," Vince repeated. "I'll tell her."

In the following silence, Arthur studied Vince's features. He couldn't recall the last time he'd seen such banked fury sparking behind his colleague's eyes. What on earth happened between the women before he joined them?

"I'll accompany her myself." Vince's clipped tone brooked no argument. "I've already told you, I'll arrange the flight. No. He'll meet you when you arrive."

Arthur flinched at the hard stare shot in his direction. Who had Vince arranged for him to meet? At first he assumed Rafe had rung to tell them Megan's little girl had been found, but he must be wrong.

"If you know what's good for you, you better be at the airport ready to get on the plane when we arrive."

Megan's push on his arm startled Arthur into giving up his place beside Vince.

"If that's Rafe I want to talk to him," Megan demanded.

Vince put his hand up, palm outwards, in a movement of negation. "No." he snapped into the receiver

"Everything is far from okay here. No, tell her yourself, she wants to speak to you."

Abruptly he passed the phone across to Megan, caught hold of Arthur's arm, and unceremoniously marched him into the spacious hallway.

Arthur watched Vince brush the back of his hand across his eyes before he spoke.

"Thanks to your manipulations, Bella is now thoroughly upset at a time when she should be feeling safe and loved. Instead, she's surrounded with aggravation, tears, shouting, and lost friendships, not to mention two frightened little girls.

"Rachel's outside sobbing her heart out because someone called her mother a liar, and Lizzie is beside Bella crying fit to bust because she's scared we won't stop Megan from taking Rachel away. And Bella, already suffering more pain than anyone should have to cope with, is worried sick and torn by divided loyalties, because Trudi's vowed to keep both you and me out of her, and I mean Trudi's, life forever."

Arthur watched Vince spin away from him, before turning back, thrusting a clenched fist under his chin.

"Didn't you ever stop to consider the repercussions before bringing Rafe here? That it might blow up in your face, and hurt everyone you claim you want to protect? I've no idea how you're going to sort this mess out, but you better start now. Because I will not tolerate losing Trudi's trust and friendship due to your thoughtless actions. We go back a long way, but I'm as close to hating you at this minute as I've ever hated anyone."

Arthur tried to protest but was interrupted before he spoke a single word.

"I've told Rafe to be ready to come back with the plane when we land. They've found Megan's daughter at his apartment, and she's now staying with Megan's mother, which means Rafe's free to return to try and sort this mess out. Make sure you're at the airport to meet him and get him back here."

"Is that wise?" Arthur managed to ask.

"Given the recent debacle, I have no idea what is wise anymore. But Trudi deserves to listen to Rafe's side of the story. Instead of memories, she lives with a blank space. Even if it turns out to be unpalatable, Trudi deserves the truth."

"What if he does try to take Rachel away from her?"

"Trudi may have told us both, in no uncertain terms, she never wants to see us again. But if you assume I'll sit back and let anyone remove Rachel from her mother, you're even more stupid than I've recently been dismayed to discover you are. And while we're at it, have Megan's luggage put in my car, while I go and collect her and tell Judy we're leaving."

And with a last hard look in his direction, Vince stalked back into the study.

ೲ

Rafe poured Scotch into a glass and pushed it across the desk to Vince. "Trudi phoned and asked me to tell you. I'm sorry about Bella."

"How did she sound?"

"Upset. Naturally. It doesn't matter how much you think you're prepared, you're still sucker-punched when you lose someone close to you."

"I was afraid something like this would happen." Vince voiced his fears aloud, shock and grief wiping the emotion from his face.

"Afraid something like what, would happen? You said it was only a matter of time." Uncertain of Vince's reaction, Rafe kept his voice neutral. Not everyone welcomed sympathy at a time of loss.

"You don't understand. Events this afternoon upset Bella. I blame myself. I should've prevented you from leaving England."

"You were hardly in a position to do that. Anyway, what difference would it make where I was this afternoon?"

"No sooner had you gone, than Megan arrived. She spotted Rachel. Of course, none of us knew how similar Rachel and Tammy are, or that Tammy had run away from home.

"Your sister virtually accused Trudi of kidnapping her daughter. Naturally, things got a bit heated between the two women before Megan showed Trudi Tammy's photograph. They look like twins, Rafe. I'm surprised you didn't notice the similarity on your arrival." Vince couldn't hide his cynicism.

"At some level, I did notice it," Rafe responded quietly. "But other impressions, that seemed more important at the time, side-tracked my attention.

"What's more important?" A sudden wave of grief hit him, and Vince raised his hand. "Don't answer. I'd better contact the airport and arrange for a return flight home."

"Stay the night. Apparently, Bella made the funeral arrangements several months ago. Trudi said everything's in hand, and there's nothing for you to do." He didn't tell Vince, Trudi had demanded Vince stayed away until the day of the funeral. No way would he keep Vince away from the Hall if he wanted to visit.

Rafe knew he'd badly misjudged Trudi for several weeks, but until today he'd never heard such bitterness in her voice. She'd demanded he keep Vince in Boston for as long as possible.

"Let Arthur handle things. It won't do you any good to go rushing back tonight. You'll be in no fit state to help anyone when you arrive."

"Arthur!" Vince spat. "Trudi won't accept any help from him either. If he hadn't interfered, none of this would have happened. And Bella might still be alive tonight," he ended on a choked sob.

"What the hell's been going on over there?"

"I told you. Your sister, mistaking Rachel for Tammy, threatened to take her away from Trudi and called her a liar. From then on, it slid downhill." Vince briefly summed up the events.

"Omigod!" Rafe combed his fingers through his hair and stared at the man sitting opposite him.

"Rafe, you have to understand. Trudi still doesn't remember anything immediately after her escape from Cadmore's house. The doctors call it 'selective amnesia.' Apparently, the longer it lasts, the less likely it is Trudi will ever recall the missing events. But we always hoped something would trigger her memory.

"We're still not sure of the exact time lapse, but at least twenty-four hours, perhaps more. And that includes no recollection of Rachel's natural father. Until she saw Tammy's photograph, Trudi hadn't noticed the resemblance between you and Rachel. Why should she? She had no reason to look for it. Now, both of them are terrified you'll try to separate them and bring Rachel back here to live with you."

"Does Trudi really believe I'd do that to her? To them?"

"You've made no secret of your contempt for her. And you also have to realize, although Trudi's faced with the probability you may be Rachel's father, she still doesn't remember what happened. As a victim of an abusive marriage for five years, I imagine Trudi is afraid Rachel is the consequence of something similar."

Rafe's face paled at the unspoken implications. "How can you be sure Cadmore isn't Rachel's father?" The idea of a daughter thrilled him and scared him witless. During the flight home, he'd blanked the possibility, convincing himself Trudi would have said something if she believed him to be her daughter's father. Now, given Vince's revelations, it seemed more than possible he did have a ten-year-old daughter.

"Wrong blood group. Rachel's blood group differs from Trudi's and Cadmore's."

"They may have mixed up the babies after the birth. It wouldn't be the first time such a mistake happened." Rafe didn't believe his own words.

"Not a chance. Trudi delivered Lizzie, and Serena delivered Rachel. Believe me, Rafe, no one mixed up in the delivery room. This is neither the time nor the place, but I'm going to insist you agree to a DNA test so we can count you in or out."

Horror washed over him as he struggled to assimilate Vince's revelations. He'd misjudged Trudi badly.

"Rafe?"

Startled, both men looked up to find his mother standing in the doorway, the light from the hall silhouetting her petite frame.

Swiftly he moved across the room and took both her hands in his. "The phone call I took before I left for the airport to meet Vince and Megan was from Arthur's sister—"

"The one whose daughter looks like Tammy?"

"Yes." Had his mother heard their conversation?

"Megan has told me what happened. Why would she want to contact you now?"

Taking his mother by the arm, Rafe led her back into the warmth of the kitchen and explained the situation, adding Trudi's demand Vince be kept away until the funeral.

"That's a bit harsh." She glanced over her shoulder toward the study. "Have you told him?"

"Of course not, what do you take me for?"

"Well how do you intend to keep him here when he can simply order up his own private plane and return back home immediately?"

"Off the top of my head, I'm going to suggest he waits for me to tidy up some business, and I'll fly back with him for the funeral. Also, he wants—" Rafe hesitated.

"What?"

"If Rachel is my daughter, I'm not walking away from her. I've agreed to a DNA test." Could this day get any worse, Rafe wondered as he looked down into his mother's worried face.

"If you agree to the test, Rafe, you do realize the consequences to this family, when your siblings discover your blood group is different from theirs?"

His mother's hand rested over his heart, as it raced into overdrive.

"Hell!" He felt the blood drain from his face as, horrified, he stared at his mother.

"What is the child's blood group?"

Rafe shook his head, shock rendering him speechless. The fact that one mindless act of pure joy could impact on so many lives, more than a decade later, appalled him. Two families could be torn apart because, for a few wonderful hours, he'd allowed lust to overrule his senses.

"What am I going to do?" He stared at his mother's shocked face. When would this nightmare end?

He owed his mother and Jess Hawk for their years' of silence and unconditional love.

Did he also owe it to his siblings to reveal the truth, and if so, at what cost?

And Rachel? Wasn't it his duty to ensure her father was willing to be around for her if she wanted him?

And what about Trudi? Didn't he owe a duty to her, too? At least to guarantee she and Rachel were both financially secure in the future. If he asked for more, would she even consider it? Rafe doubted it. Why would she agree to a marriage of convenience with him, when she'd suffered at Cadmore's hands?

She'd managed perfectly well for the past ten years, why would she accept anything from him now?

Would he, like his birth father before him, have to walk away from the woman and child in his life to uphold his duty to his family?

"Follow your heart." His mother's whispered words penetrated his painful thoughts.

For the first time in his life, Rafe sympathised with Daniel Kinsale's dilemma.

CHAPTER 9

From the edge of the patio, Trudi watched Bella's friends gather in the garden, remembering, sharing, laughing, and crying. They celebrated Bella's life rather than mourned her passing.

Her sister-in-law's verbal attack minutes ago, accusing her of selfish cowardice for not making peace with Vince and Arthur while expecting them to solve her problems had flabbergasted Trudi. She fought to contain her tears, refusing to acknowledge how the words hurt.

On top of everything else, Serena's aggression snapped Trudi's last vestige of control. She needed solitude to sort through her mangled emotions. It drove her into the house through the French doors and out through the main entrance. Casting a quick glance around to confirm no one followed her from the garden, Trudi set off, heading past the lake and along the track leading into the woods beyond.

Blackwater Farm lay about half a mile through the woods from Kinsale Hall. And since learning of Bella's intention to leave the farm to Trudi in her will, Trudi had not given the place another consideration, until today. Now she decided to satisfy her curiosity. If habitable, Trudi decided, she'd move the girls into the farmhouse within the week.

Fear churned in the pit of her stomach when she recalled the debacle following Megan's arrival the previous week. How would the subsequent revelations impact on Rachel and Lizzie if Tammy and Rachel were related? She had no idea how to deal with the situation when Rafe approached her. And he would.

After ten years of sole parenting, she'd resent Rafe's interference if he imposed his authority over both her and Rachel. Did her desire to protect the girls from any more grief brand her as insensitive and callous? Probably.

Sometime soon she'd have to research the minutiae of international parental rights and deal with her fear of losing Rachel to the novelty of a newly discovered father. One, moreover, she already liked. And what about Lizzie?

From her previous observations of the man, he treated both girls the same. But how would discovering he'd fathered one and not the other change his emotional dynamics?

Sharing Rachel with a man who held Trudi in such contempt only magnified her fears. Fears she'd have to learn to live with to give Rachel a chance to become acquainted with Rafe's side of her family. If the future proved Rafe fathered her daughter, she'd deal with it, but dear God she wondered how she'd manage.

With Bella gone, Rafe's intrusion could split the girls apart. And if the similarity between Tammy and Rachel was a strange coincidence, what then? Releasing a huff of impatience at the thoughts wind-milling through her brain, Trudi shoved open the small metal gate bordering the woods and marched through.

What happened the evening she escaped from Denny's house? She struggled to unlock the lost memories of the missing hours. So far, the key refused to turn.

Leaves crackled beneath her feet, releasing their fresh scent. Shafts of sunlight spilled between the trees lighting the path ahead, while the surrounding silence soothed her soul. The unexpected sight of a speckled fawn gazing in her direction halted her progress. Enchanted, she watched, uncertain whether it would flee for safety or not if she moved.

The gangly young deer twitched its nose, smelling the air for danger, before lowering its head and continuing to graze. How long she watched, before becoming aware of another presence, Trudi wasn't sure. But when she turned, she wasn't surprised to see Rafe standing a few feet away, studying her.

"What are you doing here?"

"We have to talk."

"I've nothing to say to you. Go away. I want to be alone."

"Where are you going?" Cautiously, Rafe moved forward.

Did he assume that like the fawn, now vanished, she too might bolt away?

"It's none of your business." Emotionally drained and feeling too tired to talk, Trudi put her hand out to repel his advance. Why couldn't he leave her alone? "Go away," she repeated, without any real hope he'd listen.

With a sigh, she watched him approach and, as if in a dream, stared as his hand wrapped gently around the top of her arm before he guided her to a nearby fallen tree trunk.

"You have nothing to fear from me." He sat at the other end of the trunk, putting some distance between them. "Did Vince tell you I've agreed to a DNA test?"

"I haven't spoken to either Vince or Arthur since your sister arrived at the Hall." No way would she admit, even to herself, how much she missed them.

"You should, you know." His voice, pitched low and soft, curled round the coldness in her heart.

"You don't know anything about it. Stay out of my affairs and go away." Appalled by the sound of tears in her voice, she turned her face away from him. The smell of crushed grass wafted on the warm air. Midges danced in the shafts of sunlight beaming to earth between the trees.

"That's not possible. If Rachel is my daughter, do you expect me to turn my back on the result of the most wonderful night of lovemaking I've ever experienced? She's a grand kid, and I'd want her to know I'm her Dad."

"Lust, Rafe. Nothing more than lust. Admit it."

"How can you be sure? Vince said you don't remember what happened."

"Oh, Vince told you, did he?" she spat at him. "How convenient! And I'm supposed to do what? Fall in line and believe what you say? Just like that? If that night was so memorable for you, how come you didn't recognize me when you arrived?

"I'm tired of other people telling me what I can, and can't do. I'm sick of being manipulated by people I trusted. And I particularly resent being told I'm a coward and brought it all on myself."

"Don't be silly. No one would think that."

"No? You don't know the half of it?" Tear's forgotten, she swung round and nearly collided with Rafe's chest. "Not half-an-hour ago, someone decided to enlighten me. My brother considers I deserved everything that happened to me since I flouted his wishes and married Denny."

"I don't believe you." Genuine shock filled his eyes.

"Believe! They accused me of carrying on like a self-centered, spoiled child who wouldn't listen when Arthur tried to warn me away from Denny. And I still can't manage my life without running to Arthur and Vince for help. I'm still relying on others to rescue me from the mess I've made of my life."

She watched the dull red stain sweep up Rafe's neck and into his face. Though he may not have voiced those hurtful words, he clearly agreed with her sister-in-law's opinion, which explained his attitude. How could he expect her to share Rachel when he held her in contempt? It couldn't work.

"I see they're not alone in their accusations." Wearily, she stood and walked away. "Go home, Rafe, Rachel is mine, and I won't have you trying to tear us apart. If you do, I'll set my own charges against you."

"You're wrong, Trudi. Rachel, if she is my child, has cousins, aunts, uncles and grandparents who want to meet her. And you're not entitled to deprive her of them."

She heard Rafe approach before he caught up with her and snared her arm again, swinging her round to face him. She watched the pulse throb in his throat and noticed his eyes darken with emotion.

"How will you explain that to Rachel when she discovers you've deprived her of such a large part of her family inheritance? How do you suppose she'll feel about you?" Rafe's hand fell away from her arm, and he stood back. "If you try to deny Rachel the right to meet the rest of her family, perhaps the person who called you a coward is right."

Shock ripped through her. If he'd punched her in the gut, his words couldn't have inflicted more pain. Would the nightmare never end?

"I see." She forced the words between clenched teeth. "Now I know how you feel, at least I know where I stand."

"What's that supposed to mean?"

"Anything you like, Rafe. After all, you're the one with the memories, but I'm the one with a daughter. And I won't let you take Rachel away from me. I'll fight you to hell and back before I let you split Lizzie and Rachel apart simply to satisfy your desire to play at daddies. In fact, I'll die before you can do that."

"Stop being so melodramatic, Trudi, and sit down and listen to me," Rafe roared at her.

She ducked, and unconsciously rubbed her arm where Rafe had held her.

"Please?" he asked.

The contrasting gentleness in his voice drained the fight from her. Fatigue gnawed at the fringes of her mind, numbing her thought process. Perhaps she should sit down for a few moments, before she fell down.

His long fingers stretched out toward her. She noticed how the blond hairs on the back of his hand disappeared beneath the cuff of his light blue silk shirt. The musky scent of his aftershave sent shivers down her spine. For the first time, Trudi noticed Rafe had loosened his tie. Why did her heart flutter at the sight? Silently, she sat down on the log again. Weariness threatened, and her emotions were in turmoil. It couldn't hurt to sit down for a few moments.

She let Rafe settle beside her and pull her up against his chest. His muscles rippled as his arms wrapped around her. The warmth from his chest soothed, and she allowed her eyes to close against the sun for a moment.

crocro

The surrounding sounds of the woodland faded as
Rafe reflected on Trudi's revelation. Who'd accused her of
cowardice? He didn't believe it. She'd misunderstood.
During the last few days back home, he'd analysed his
feelings for her and wondered why he'd been so eager to
find fault with her.

Gently, he brushed his lips across her hair and
considered Vince's question last week. The same one Trudi
had thrown at him. How come he'd not recognized Trudi
when he'd first arrived at the Hall?

He looked down at the exhausted woman sleeping in
his arms and saw the pallor of her skin and the dark
smudges beneath her eyes. Her sun-dried tears had left salty
tracks down her cheeks. For the first time he focussed
beyond his own desire to become acquainted with his
daughter and acknowledged the fear Trudi must be feeling
for her family's uncertain future.

Carefully, he straddled the tree trunk and pulled
Trudi's sleeping form more firmly against him.

He remembered resisting the extraordinary soul
connection when they met. Had he been subliminally aware
of the long association between them even then? The
mature, voluptuous woman, who'd greeted Arthur so many
weeks ago, bore no resemblance to the gray-skinned,
drawn, and underweight woman who'd saved his life then

drawn him in after their incredible rescue from the flood-swollen river.

He'd still missed the connection, even after her admission about inheriting Kinsale Hall from her husband. After all, Cadmore wagered his sister not his wife during the game. Until Arthur told him the following morning, how was Rafe to appreciate the man lied?

In hindsight, it staggered him to realize he hadn't recognized Arthur's hand behind the commission to design the chalets.

Finding himself face to face with Dennis Cadmore's widow had colored his judgement. He brushed away a stray curl from Trudi's face. Would she believe him when he told her he wanted to be a permanent part of her life? A cold band of fear clamped his heart at the thought of never seeing Trudi or Rachel again. He forced his mind into more mundane directions, such as where Trudi had been heading.

Rafe had been present for the reading of Bella's will and knew she'd left her friend an adjoining property. Had Trudi planned to look at the place now? No one had mentioned the trespasser recently, and the idea of her wandering around alone disturbed him.

Perhaps he could persuade her to accept his company when she woke. He'd noticed the dark circles under her eyes when he'd arrived and seen her haunted expression earlier. Everyone affected by the recent revelations had been shocked. But for Trudi, the additional fear of the unknown must be intolerable. Did she believe he'd try to take Rachel away from her? He'd never do that to either of them, but he did intend to stick around in their lives and be an integral part of their future. And while he wasn't sure how Trudi would react, he hoped to convince her to marry him.

While she slept in his arms, Rafe ran through his options and watched the sun begin to sink behind the trees. Soon he would have to wake his sleeping beauty.

ひとつ

Weaving between the mourners, Arthur made his way across the grass to join his wife. "Have you seen Trudi?"

"Not since we spoke about an hour ago. Why?"

Surprised by Serena's belligerent tone, Arthur studied her pale face in silence. "What happened between the two of you?"

"What makes you think something happened?"

"Serena, my love, after our years together, I recognize when you're upset. So, tell me."

"She asked if you were all right."

"And that upset you?"

"Well, of course, it did. When she carries on like a spoiled child, telling everyone who's been there for her since Rachel's birth, she doesn't want anything more to do with them, of course, I'm upset. What did you expect?

"For the past week, you've gone around like a lost soul. Do you expect me to sit quietly on the side lines while you're hurting? I told her a few home truths, and like the spoiled brat the woman is, she's gone off to sulk."

"I thought you liked her."

"I did—I do—But she's hurt you, and I won't forgive her. Why should she get away with that, when you've gone out of your way to do so much for her? You even tried to stop her from seeing Denny Cadmore, for God's sake! If she'd listened to you, none of the rest of this would have happened."

"You didn't say that to her? Please, tell me you didn't say that," Arthur pleaded.

"Of course, I did." Serena placed a comforting hand on her husband's chest.

"You've got it wrong. I admit, at the time I acted with the best of intentions, but my actions drove my sister away."

"Don't be silly Arthur. Trudi wanted her own way and refused to listen to your advice. If she'd listened—"

"You mean well, and I appreciate your loyalty, but this time it's misplaced. We were sixteen when Cadmore made a play for Trudi. He recognized her vulnerability, and knowing his reputation, I forbade her to go out with him.

"The more control I applied, the more she rebelled. I may have acted out of love, but I should have found another way to handle her. In assuming the heavy-handed role of parent to a sibling minutes younger than myself, I drove her right into the arms of the man I wanted to keep her safe from. Trudi didn't run to Cadmore. She ran away from me and the control I persisted on exerting. And I've had to live with that ever since."

"But you were only sixteen, Arthur. You'd recently lost your parents in the plane crash. Of course, you wanted to protect your sister."

"They were her parents too, Serena. Like me, her grief probably controlled her actions and reactions, just as mine did. You can't excuse one of us, without doing the same for both."

Arthur felt Serena's head rest on his shoulder and her arms tighten around his waist. He dropped a gentle kiss on her hair. "And now," he added grimly, "my interference is creating suffering for people I've never met."

"What are you talking about? What have you done?"

"I've long suspected Rafe may be Rachel's father so when Trudi asked if I'd recommend someone to design the chalets, I persuade Rafe to take the commission."

Serena pulled away from his shoulder, the color leaching from her face. "Are you telling me you deliberately orchestrated the meeting between them this summer? That you—that I—Omigod, what have I done? I told her— She'll never forgive me. Oh God, I have to find her."

"It's better you leave her alone. I'm sure once she calms down, Trudi will realize you never meant what you said."

"Surely someone should search for her, I hate to think how isolated I've made her feel, especially with Bella gone, and falling out with all of us." Tears brimmed over and trickled down her cheeks.

Arthur handed Serena his large white hanky to dry her eyes. "Rafe went into the house a while ago, and he's not returned. Perhaps he's with her. In the meantime, I suggest you fix a smile in place and help me encourage everyone to head for home." He tapped the tip of her nose. "Until Trudi joins us, I suggest we stay with the girls. They were playing with Judy, last time I saw them."

Arthur turned when Vince approached, his mobile phone clamped to his ear.

"Don't go any closer to the building and make sure Trudi is safe." Vince joined them and mouthed for them to wait while he listened to the voice on the other end of the call. "No, don't approach on your own. I'll call for back-up. We need to make sure he doesn't get away from us. I'm bringing Arthur with me." He snapped his phone shut.

"Rafe followed Trudi to Blackwater Farm where they've disturbed an intruder. All the signs indicate someone's been living at the farm. We've tracked down our trespasser, and it's Bella's ex. Come on Arthur, we need to get over there.

"I'm sorry to take Arthur away, Serena, but we've got to protect Lizzie. We think he intends to kidnap her. Please try to persuade everyone to leave. We don't need any unforeseen accidents around here. Oh, and make sure the girls remain indoors. If necessary, ask Judy to stay with them." Vince pulled out his phone again, barked some orders, then returned it to his pocket.

"The police are on their way. Arthur, do you know whether Roger Frobisher is here? I saw Alice in the kitchen earlier but not her husband. We could use him. Have you brought a weapon?"

Arthur patted his jacket.

∞∞∞

Out of nowhere, dust spat up from the ground inches in front of Rafe's feet. His glance at the overhead branches. They revealed nothing that would impact the ground hard enough to kick up dust. A whizzing sound close to his ear galvanised Rafe into action. He pushed Trudi to the ground and rolled to a crouching position behind a nearby bush, pulling her with him, before grabbing his cell phone.

"Didn't you realize anyone was living here?" he asked as he dialled.

"No one said anything about a tenant." Trudi crawled closer to the bush and nearer to Rafe.

"This guy's not a regular tenant," Rafe muttered. "What possible motive would he have for shooting at someone approaching the building, unless he's using the place without permission?"

"Do you think this is where our trespasser is living?"

Rafe's heart skipped a beat at Trudi's possessive term to describe the man in the farmhouse. Certain he'd seen the outline of a man standing at the window a split second before the first shot, Rafe nodded.

"Vince says," he said, lowering his phone from his ear, "it's Bella's ex. But why would he be hanging around here after all these years?"

Trudi turned her gaze toward the farmhouse and drew her knees up under her chin before she spoke.

"Like me, Bella was in an abusive marriage. When she fell pregnant with Lizzie, her husband beat her up in an attempt to induce a miscarriage. Bella escaped but he found her a couple of weeks later. There's no point in going into details, but suffice to say she didn't dare try to leave again. When her contractions started he drove her to the hospital and told her he'd be right back and not to try and do anything stupid, like leaving.

"She never saw him again. When Lizzie turned two, he began sending Bella explicit letters, threatening both her life and Lizzie's. With Arthur and Vince's help, he was eventually sentenced to twelve years inside. I suppose he got out early. If he is in the farmhouse, I presume he's after Lizzie's inheritance. Nothing else makes sense."

"How did the two of you meet?" Rafe chanced a quick glance toward the farmhouse. Pale sunlight glinted on metal at an upper window and disappeared.

"We met at the hospital when we were expecting and arranged to go to the same classes together and coach each other. But then Lizzie and Rachel decided to arrive at the same time, and we ended up in the same delivery room together."

Rafe recalled Vince's remark about Trudi delivering Lizzie but made no comment. Right now they had other things to deal with. He poked his head round the bush and quickly pulled back again as another bullet whizzed past and kicked up dust a few feet away. If they tried to retreat, they might get hurt. And with no cover between the bush and the farmhouse, they'd have no chance to get any closer. He pulled out his cell phone and briefly updated Vince.

The shadows lengthened, and Rafe slipped his jacket over Trudi's shoulders. Earlier, while she slept, her scent had tickled his mind, a mixture of soap and fresh flowers. Now it reached him again, the fragrance of her shampoo teasing his consciousness and scattering his thoughts. He brushed his lips across the softness of her hair and marvelled at her composure under fire.

I love you. When had love become an issue? Yes he wanted to marry Trudi, because it was more expedient for him to look after her and the girls, but it had nothing to do with love. Did it?

The memory of his conversation with his mother a few months ago taunted him. *'Love at first sight happens.'* When had it snuck up on him? How had Trudi burrowed beneath his rigid independence his need to control his life? He angled his head to look at the woman beside him. Had his immediate antipathy and resentment against Trudi been the flip-side of love, and he'd unconsciously fought the inevitable? He wanted to run, he wanted to stay. And he discovered with amazement, he wanted to stay more than he wanted to run.

His heart lifted at the notion of sharing a home with Trudi and the two girls. Now he'd made it, his decision to ask Trudi to marry him seemed right. The enormity of his task fired his blood. Just because he'd finally acknowledged his true feelings for her didn't guarantee he'd persuade her to recognize how good they'd be together.

Movement at the edge of the wood caught his attention. He nudged Trudi's arm and inclined his head. "The cavalry has arrived."

A shot to their left followed by the sound of shattering glass confirmed Rafe's assumption. Followed by another shot, near the woods this time, then several uniformed officers began zigzagging toward the farmhouse.

"Stay here until we are sure he's disarmed." Arthur crouched beside them.

Trudi touched his arm lightly, curling her fingers round his wrist. "Please, be careful." Tears slid down her face.

Arthur hunkered down beside her, thumbed the tears away with a brief kiss on her cheek, and prepared to move on. "Don't worry, Trudi. You don't think I'd let anything happen before we've had a chance to talk, do you?" With a swift glance at Rafe, he said, "Keep her down until we're sure we've secured the situation. Then get her the hell out of here. Serena's frantic with worry." He saw Trudi stiffen. "She didn't mean what she said. You have to believe me. Please don't hold it against her."

A shout from the house alerted Arthur it was safe for him to approach. "Get her away from here. Now! Go," he urged and was gone.

"Come on. You heard the guy. Let's get out of here."
Rafe pulled Trudi to her feet and began running, towing her
behind him.

"What if he gets hurt?" Trudi gasped when they
reached the shelter of the trees. "We had a terrible row.
And I'll never forgive myself if anything happens to him."

"Come on, Trudi. He's been doing this kind of work
for years. You should be used to it by now." He slowed his
pace when the trees protected them.

"I don't think I'll ever get used to it," she replied. "We
were sixteen when I left home. The next time we met, he
was already engaged to Serena. When they lost their first
child he gave up field work to stay home with her. He was
still working away when we were becoming reacquainted,
so I never saw much of him. And then as a new mother, I
had other things on my mind."

"You'll never know how sorry I am, I wasn't there for
you. This isn't the time to talk, but we will later. And I'm
hoping you won't push me away. You have nothing to fear
from me. I promise you."

Unaware he held his breath, Rafe watched the
emotions flit across her face. With a tentative smile, she
nodded her head. The air whooshed out of his lungs.

Discovering he could suddenly empathise with Daniel
Kinsale's dilemma—if not his decision to return home to
his wife and estates, leaving behind the woman he loved
and his unborn child—astonished Rafe beyond belief. The
irony of his present position was not lost on him.

He ducked his head, and set off in the direction of the Hall, leaving Trudi to follow.

%ンゴ

"Shit!" Vince stared down at the body, flung back against a wall splattered with blood. Even with half of the man's face missing, Vince positively identified his former brother-in-law. "The amount of paperwork this jerk's going to cost us is unbelievable, let alone the inevitable enquiry. This," Vince said, waving angrily toward the corpse, "means I'm going to have to return to the office. Tell Trudi I'll let her know when she can come back here. Until then, ask her to stay away until I give the all-clear."

"Sure. Do you want me to join you?" Arthur gazed at the empty beer cans and fast food wrappers scattered across the floor. Candles sat on upturned empty tins, with a lighter and box of matches sitting near a thick sleeping bag on the floor. Had Bella's ex known about the funeral today? A quick search through the house indicated the man had been around for some time, and intended to stay a while longer.

A torn curtain fluttered at the smashed window, and Arthur studied Rafe and Trudi's meager shelter.

The ferocity with which his plans ran out of control appalled Arthur. How could his best intentions go haywire? With no chance to talk, he had no idea how Rafe's family reacted to the revelations about Trudi and Rachel.

Would she stonewall Serena when she reached the Hall? He hoped not. There'd been enough misunderstandings to last a lifetime, without having to deal with the two women tip-toeing around each other forever more. He'd felt heartened to notice Trudi hadn't pushed Rafe's supporting arm away when they headed for safety.

He just wished he knew Rafe's intentions regarding her.

CHAPTER 10

"I'm sorry, Trudi. I didn't mean it." Stunned, Trudi braced herself against Serena's tearful hug. "Please tell me you forgive me. It upset me to see Arthur hurting after your quarrel."

"It doesn't matter. It always helps to find out what someone thinks about you." Trudi failed to conceal the lingering bitterness of her sister-in-law's unexpected attack. And right now her reaction to becoming a gunman's target, on top of everything else, threatened to deck her where she stood.

"That's not fair." Serena inhaled deeply.

Trudi cut her off before she continued. "Who said anything about fairness?" Struggling to hold onto her disintegrating composure, Trudi placed her hands on her sister-in-law's shoulders and pushed her away. "You stated your opinion clearly. And I received it loud and clear. You'll have to excuse me. I need to find my daughters."

"That wasn't very gracious of you." Startled, Trudi swung round to find Rafe beside her.

"You're right. Gracious is the last thing I'm feeling right now. Lonely, frightened, inadequate are a few of my emotions. Why not tack on 'ungracious' to the end of the others?"

"You're upset right now—"

"You don't know anything, Rafe. Leave me alone. Go back and tell everyone what a gallant hero you've been this afternoon." The vindictive words kept rolling off her tongue before Trudi managed to stop them. Humiliation consumed her as she listened to herself.

Serena's attack, coming on top of everything else, destroyed her sense of family identity. Overcoming a strong desire to go in search of a dark and quiet corner, Trudi pulled her shoulders back and retraced her steps. Sometimes a person's actions hurt, but did she have the right to condemn Serena for speaking from her heart?

"I'm sorry if I misjudged you. It's okay, Serena. I do understand. But now I need to be with my girls." Giving her sister-in-law a brief hug, Trudi spun on her heels and went in search of her daughters. She needed to reassure them she'd be there for them to provide comfort and cuddles. They relied on her to present an air of serenity during their grief.

She splashed her face with cold water and freshened her light makeup, before heading for Rachel's room to find the children playing with a new video game Rafe brought back with him from Boston. The sound of their laughter and exclamations of delight cheered her battered soul. Grateful the girls were enjoying themselves, Trudi lay back in the chair near the window, rested her head against the soft cushions, closed her eyes, and let the memories in.

Six months pregnant and waiting for her regular check-up, Trudi hadn't noticed Bella's entrance until the new arrival literally tripped over the table in the center of the room and landed in her lap. They'd bonded instantly, and nothing had separated them. Until last week.

The house seemed so empty without Bella's presence and quiet strength. For eleven years they'd done everything together. They'd shared their tears and fears, their joys and laughter. Now, Trudi accepted that Rachel and Lizzie depended on her strength to help them through the next days and weeks. In Bella's memory, Trudi determined she would not fail them.

Swiping at the tears tracking down her cheeks from beneath her closed lashes, she berated herself for her show of weakness. Lizzie needed her to be strong, needed to trust Trudi to be there for her and Rachel. And confirming the arrangements Bella had made for the three of them to enjoy a holiday break together after the funeral needed her attention first thing in the morning.

When they returned, she intended to move into Blackwater Farm. Duty had its place and time. And she considered her duty to Kinsale Hall ended the day she lost her best friend.

Peter Jenkins, the estate manager, would continue his competent running of the Hall's affairs wherever Trudi lived. When she and the girls moved to the farm, she'd be close enough to meet with Peter regularly and discuss estate matters.

Over time her accountancy business had grown steadily, and now her list of clients comprised several local retailers, including the local gallery where the owner displayed some of her paintings. The woman put outrageously high prices on them and sold them easily. Trudi could easily transfer both her business and her painting to Blackwater Farm.

Abruptly, her musing skittered to a halt. She had bigger problems. Because of Arthur's meddling, she risked losing Rachel to strangers in another country.

She had to assume Rafe was lying when he promised not to fight for custody. Why wouldn't he? He was a natural with the children. And how had she missed the likeness between him and Rachel? Why had no one else noticed the similarity between them?

The hairs on the back of her neck tingled, and she looked up to see Rafe standing in the open doorway. How long had he been watching her? Why didn't he leave her alone and give her time to adjust to the recent traumas in her life? She wished he'd go away, but knew he wouldn't any more now than he had this afternoon when he'd caught up with her in the woods.

"Is something wrong?"

"No." Rafe walked across the room and sat on the side of her chair, resting his arm along the back.

His warmth radiated up her neck and down her spine. Her hands trembled with the need to comb their way through his hair. Her body wanted to drown in the depth of his hazy gray gaze. Her breasts tightened and grew taught and the pull of inner heat consumed her thoughts, frightening her in its intensity. No one else stirred these emotions. Trudi turned her face and felt his lips softly caress her forehead. She jerked away like a frightened rabbit, her eyes large and dark.

"I wish to God, things had been different between us." At his muttered oath, the girls swivelled round from the screen holding their attention.

"Hi, Rafe, come and join us," they implored.

"Not now. I need to steal your Mom away for a few moments."

Trudi noticed the crinkle of laugh lines radiating from the corners of his eyes when he leaned down to ruffle the girls' hair.

"Okay." As one, they smiled at Rafe then refocused on their computer game. He entwined his fingers through Trudi's and pulled her up from her chair and out of the room.

"Is there somewhere we can go where we won't be interrupted?"

Trudi shook her head. She wanted to unscramble the feelings this man evoked. It wouldn't do to forget he was not her friend. "Not now. I've been away from the guests too long as it is. I'd better go back."

"What's between us isn't going to go away. Sooner or later, we have to discuss it."

His determination slammed into her heart.

She wanted to yell, '*You may be right, but until we have some irrefutable evidence, I don't have to do anything. I suggest you take yourself off with Arthur and Serena tonight and leave me and the girls alone.*' But she swallowed her instinct and said instead, "Later. This is not the time to discuss this." The ebb and flow of people in the garden mirrored her life, Trudi mused.

She shifted to face Rafe again. "I can admit this may not seem fair to you, but I'm not feeling rational at the moment. And I need a clear head for something this important."

"Very well. But this isn't going to go away."

Too afraid to say anything more, Trudi nodded and headed outside.

ೀೀೀ

Rafe's raised voice startled Trudi into immobility on her return to the den.

"The results won't be in for another ten days, Arthur. I'm not prepared to waste that time in allowing her to build barriers against me. I'm staying here."

Rafe's anger barrelled through the doorway and hit Trudi squarely between the eyes. The now familiar sense of resentment flared. Who did he think he was riding rough-shod over everyone, always determined to get his own way? Swiftly she moved into the den.

"You can please yourself where you stay, Rafe, but it won't be here. Do I make myself clear? Your sister may have seen fit to create allegations against me. But until they are proved beyond doubt, you'll stay away from me. Unless you want me to have you charged with stalking. Or worse."

Only the sound of her angry breathing filled the stunned silence that followed her tirade.

"Trudi, we need time to get to know each other—"

"Wrong again, Rafe," she spat. "I neither *need* nor *have* to do anything that involves you until you show me proof otherwise." Trudi glanced at Arthur and Serena, quietly observing the two of them. "Arthur's your friend. Stay with him."

"I'm your friend too, Trudi." His soft tone whispered across her senses drawing her in. How she wanted to believe him.

"No. You're not my friend. That doesn't mean I didn't appreciate your support and help this afternoon at the farm. But you're my enemy, not my friend. And I'll not forget that, even if you can."

"Trudi—" Rafe moved forward, his hand outstretched.

Trudi pushed her arms behind her back. "You don't even like me, Rafe. In my book that doesn't describe the actions of a friend. Once more I'll ask you. Go away. Go away and leave us alone. And," she added vehemently, "don't try to buy my girls or turn them against me." Shaking with fear and anger, Trudi rushed from the room.

Did Rafe think he could simply whisk Rachel across the Atlantic to meet her new family without repercussions? And did he truly expect her to believe that if Rachel turned out to be his daughter, he wouldn't try to keep her there once she left England? If he thought she'd believe that, he must assume she was a fool.

She had to give the whole issue some serious consideration. Rafe had rights, and whether she liked it or not she'd have to address them. Tackle and overcome her fears of abandonment.

Asking Arthur for help was out of the question. His friendship with Rafe prevented that. Besides he would tell her she needed a man in her life. Perhaps he had a point, but not without love. And love had betrayed her too often in the past for her to believe it held the key to her future now. Besides, love didn't figure in Rafe's demands.

Had Serena spoken the truth after all? Did she rely too much on Arthur and Vince? Perhaps, Trudi conceded. Had her ever-present resentment of being manipulated to take on Kinsale Hall been used to punish the two men by relying on them to ease her problems? She hadn't seen it that way. All the more reason for her to deal with Rafe's threats alone.

Trusting others hadn't served her in the past. Loving meant losing.

With Rachel, and now Lizzie, it was different. Their love would last into the future.

Unconditional.

Unencumbered.

For as long as they needed her, she would be there for them both. No one else mattered.

When she returned to them, Rachel and Lizzie clamoured for just one more game, and pestered Trudi to let them stay up much longer than their usual bedtime. For once she let them play with their computer game until unable to stay awake any longer. Then she carried them up to their rooms and tucked them into bed.

છબ્ઝ

When Rafe walked into the kitchen the following morning, Trudi was pouring cereal into the girl's bowls.

"Morning, ladies. May I join you?"

She fetched the milk from the fridge and handed it to Lizzie. "I thought you were leaving last night?" Where had he slept?

"As you can see, I'm still here."

His tone may have been quiet for the benefit of the watching girls, but his eyes bored deep into her psyche. She acknowledged the implacability in them. The distant sound of her phone ringing in the study distracted her.

"Help yourself." With a wide sweep of her arm she indicated the cereal on the surface behind her and dashed from the room.

♥♥♥

Rafe's eyes narrowed when she re-entered with a smug smile.

"Time to pack, girls. We're off tomorrow morning."

He watched the chairs tumble backwards when Rachel and Lizzie flew into Trudi's arms.

"We're truly going to Disney Land?" Laughing and crying, they whooped around the room, waving their arms in the air.

"Yes, we truly are going. And that means an early night tonight because we have to leave here in the dark tomorrow morning if we're to catch the plane on time."

How the hell had she managed to get a booking so quickly and easily? Rafe saw his opportunity to get close to Trudi disappearing before his eyes. "How'd you manage that?"

"I didn't." Trudi smiled. "Bella arranged everything months ago. I promised her I wouldn't let them hang around the house and mope. We always dreamed of going together, and when it became apparent it wouldn't happen, Bella made me promise to take the girls as soon as possible after…"

He watched her swallow her grief and hitch her shoulders back before turning to the girls.

"When you've finished here, go and start sorting out what you want to take with you. Remember you can't take everything," she told them with a smile.

Rafe couldn't fault her there. She made an excellent mother. Rachel and Lizzie were both wonderful children.

Trudi's pleasure at the idea of escaping his presence for a few days annoyed him. "How long will you be gone?" Could he possibly organise a ticket to Paris? He'd try if it killed him.

"Ten days. We had no way of knowing when we could honor the booking. Luckily Miss Taverham, their headmistress, agreed to give them time off school if the bookings fell in term time." Trudi wiped the surfaces clean and replaced the washed pots in the cupboards. "Fortunately, they'll only miss a couple of days of the new term. That reminds me, I better phone her while it's in my mind."

"You haven't eaten. You shouldn't skip meals." Rafe moved across the room and held the kettle under the cold-water tap. "If you're going gadding all over the place, you need to keep your strength up." He derived a perverse sense of enjoyment in knowing his words would irritate her. He refused to admit she'd angered him with this unexpected holiday plan.

"Tea? Coffee?" He searched through the cupboards until he found the canisters.

"Neither, thanks." He watched her grab a glass and fill it from the cold tap before gulping down the contents. "I have to make arrangements with Judy and the Frobishers while we're away."

Rafe blocked her exit before Trudi left. "Well, remember this while you're gone. By the time you get back, I'll have the results of my DNA test. And I'll be waiting when you return." He lifted a crooked finger and chucked her under the chin.

Seeing the fear in her eyes almost destroyed him. He swooped down and caught her lips beneath his. "If you try, we can make things work between us. You want me, you know you do. And I'll admit you're disturbing my sanity. I want you so much, I can't remember when I last had a full night's sleep. We'd be good together in bed."

"Lust, Rafe." He noticed the color drain from her face. "Lust is not enough, and I won't risk my girls because you still can't control your hormones." With that, she walked round him, leaving him standing in the empty kitchen, shocked to the core.

෴

Once booked into the hotel, it didn't take Rafe long to discover Trudi and the girls had adjoining rooms on the floor below. Searching for them in the Park was out of the question. Instead, he spent the day on the phone to his office and contractors. In the evening, Rafe headed down to Trudi's room. The children's excited chatter cut off when he knocked on their door.

"Come in." Rafe realized they assumed he was delivering room service, and knocked again. After a pause that seemed like eternity, the door opened. Trudi stood before him. Shock drained the windswept roses from her cheeks and dulled the brightness in her eyes. The hand holding the door shifted in an attempt to close it his face. With the flat of his hand, Rafe prevented her from doing so.

Glancing beyond her shoulder, he spied Rachel and Lizzie watching them.

"May I come in?" The aroma of chicken and fries wafted across the room, and he noticed the white, grease splotched, paper towel crumpled in Trudi's fingers. Keeping his gaze focussed on hers, Rafe gently swiped a shard of chicken from the fullness of her lower lip and licked it off the tip of his finger while keeping his smoky gray gaze locked with hers.

"Umm, delicious." His lips curved into a boyish smile, deepening the dimple in his left cheek.

"You want some of mine?" Rachel lifted her container of chicken toward him in offering.

"Sure, pumpkin, I'll help you out if you're stuck there." Walking round Trudi, he crossed the thick cream colored pile carpet, and perched on the arm of Rachel's chair. He dipped two fingers into her chips, lifted one out and held it beneath his nose inhaling deeply before releasing a heartfelt sigh. "I've waited all day for one of these," he joked, delighted to set the girls giggling at his silly antics. Trudi sat on the floor, leaning back beside Lizzie. Her loose flowing denim shirt contrasted with the rich chintzy pattern of the sofa.

"Did you have a good day?" Rafe asked.

For the next hour he listened to the girls relate their adventures in Disneyland starting with their breakfast with Micky and the rides they'd been on.

"The crowds almost crushed us, so we didn't stay for the parade." Rachel explained. "Mum said we could try again tomorrow. Would you like to come with us?"

"Yeah, I'd like that." Rafe smiled at Rachel, "Perhaps I can help with the crowd control."

"I wish Mum was here to share it with us."

Rafe caught Lizzie's bleak gaze and opened his arms for her to crawl onto his lap. He felt the warmth of her soft cheek nestle into the curve of his neck as a sob racked her body. His hand caressed Lizzie's back in soothing strokes.

"I know, hon." His arms closed around her.

He recognized the girl's grief mirrored in Trudi's eyes. He wished he could wrap her in his arms too and kiss away her sadness. Rachel moved nearer to her mother. It struck him that a stranger walking into the room might easily mistake them for a family. The soft glow of the lamp cast a warm halo of light around them, creating an enclosed little world of their own, not open to intruders.

"They're both tired. We've been on the go since early this morning. They were so excited at the idea of breakfasting with Micky, they hardly slept last night."

Trudi's soft tone drifted across her daughter's head now resting in sleep on her mother's shoulder. "I better get them both to bed."

"I'll stay with Lizzie while you help Rachel." He wasn't going to give her a chance to refuse his offer by asking. "Go on," Rafe urged. "We'll be fine. Lizzie's asleep too." He angled his head to look at the now sleeping child in his arms. "Go on," he repeated softly.

Later, when Trudi returned after settling both girls for the night, Rafe offered her a glass of wine. "You look beat yourself."

"Well, thanks for the kind words."

Her soft smile reached into his heart. Would she ever learn to trust him enough to believe in a good future together? He noticed the faint tinge of color in her cheeks and the dark smudges beneath her eyes. Her apparent fragility masked her strength and determination to keep her independence.

With a laugh, Rafe took one of Trudi's hands, led her across the room, and gently pushed her onto the sofa before kneeling on the floor in front of her. When her eyes widened in surprise he noticed flecks of darker brown in the golden amber sheen. He sat back on his haunches and took one of her feet between his hands and began massaging.

"Mmm." Her eyes closed in bliss. "That is so…I can't put into words how good it feels." Trudi leaned back into the cushions. "Where did you learn to do this?"

"When I was at college one of my room-mates studied reflexology and practiced on me. Before her exams I used to help her through her revisions. I guess I picked up enough of the technical information to understand how the massage relates to the rest of the body. When my mother broke her shoulder in a skiing accident, I used it to help with her pain relief and relaxation."

"No wonder you're good."

Rafe shifted to Trudi's other foot and repeated the methodical strokes and massage, working each point in turn. When her breathing indicated she slept, he continued the rhythmical movements for several moments before moving up to circle his fingers round her ankle and then stilled. He couldn't change the past. Starting tomorrow he'd work to influence the future.

Rafe carefully lifted Trudi off the sofa, carried her to her bed, and covered her with the pale peach sheet. When he returned to the living area, he cleared away the remains of their meal.

Returning to his empty room didn't appeal. A glance through the window revealed heavy rain beating on the glass. Picking up the TV remote, he settled on the sofa and, keeping the volume low, tuned into an old American movie. Unaware of sleep overtaking him, he never heard the remote drop on the floor.

CHAPTER 11

Rafe woke before dawn the following morning and turned off the TV before returning to his room. He crashed into his own bed until the girls, pounding on his door a couple of hours later, startled him awake. Brimming with excitement, they urged him to hurry or he'd be too late to join them.

The entire holiday turned into a roaring success—filled with laughter and shared experiences he'd hoped would become shared memories. After four action-packed days at Disneyland, they travelled to Paris and signed in at the pre-arranged lodgings. The hoped-for invitation to join them never came, so he found a room not too far away.

They explored the magic of Paris. Both girls sat while a talented street artist drew their portraits and enchanted them when he blew them kisses while he worked. With arms around each other they giggled and laughed and asked for translation when he broke into a stream of rapid French. The girls blushed when Trudi interpreted for them.

They took a boat trip down the Seine. And when they visited cathedrals and monuments, Rafe expected it to bore the girls. Instead, Trudi's stories brought the history of each place alive. Rafe listened as the girls bombarded her with questions. When Trudi didn't have the answer, she created a treasure hunt environment, resulting in the girls competing to come up with the information first.

His respect for Trudi grew. She accepted his presence as inevitable, neither promoting him to the girls, nor generating a hostile atmosphere between them. But she never quite dropped her guard.

And in a nano-second, the sight of his parents waiting at the top of the steps when they arrived home, dashed his hopes to the ground and robbed him of the progress he'd made with Trudi during the last ten days.

"Who are they?" She cast a puzzled frown in his direction, the color draining from her cheeks when she made the connection. "You know them, don't you?"

Rafe nodded. "My parents."

Her instant withdrawal chilled him to the bone. Her bright eyes frosted over as her hands fisted in her lap and her gaze flew to her daughter.

"I see." Her flat tone sliced through the air.

Everything they'd shared in Paris was soured with suspicions. She climbed from the cab without a backward glance and left him to retrieve their cases.

Rafe loved his parents dearly, but at this moment wished them on the planet Zog. Buying time, he moved to the driver's window, paid the fare, and watched the cab disappear down the wide sweeping curve of the drive until it vanished from sight.

He turned to discover his step-father lifting one of the larger cases. "It's uncanny, Rafe, I can understand why Megan flipped the first time she caught sight of Rachel." Jess's low tone trembled with emotion.

Revealing more than he knew, Rafe turned to him. "It's good to see you, but why are you here?"

"Not to cause trouble," Jess responded quickly.

"Maybe not," Rafe sighed. "But you have none-the-less. Trudi's terrified I'm going to sue for custody and move Rachel to Boston. In her eyes, your presence here will only validate her fears. I love you both dearly, but, oh God, why did you have to arrive now?"

Rafe kneaded his neck with two fingers, watching Trudi rest a hand on the shoulder of each girl as she approached his mother at the top of the steps. He recognized from the rigid stance of her body that she'd present the "I'm master of my world" face to her perceived enemy. Trudi bent and spoke too quietly to the girls for him to hear. Then she lifted one hand from Rachel's shoulder and extended it toward his mother.

A gentle breeze lifted her curls and brushed them across her face. Trudi shook the random strands out of her eyes before turning to introduce Rachel and Lizzie to Martha Hawk. A few more words passed between the women before Trudi ushered the girls inside and disappeared from view.

His mother moved toward the door, stopped and turned blindly to face the two men at the foot of the steps her lips forming an astonished O! "She's...she's..."

Rafe watched his mother shake her head.

"Yes." He took the steps two at a time and clasped her small hand in his. "But first and foremost Rachel is Trudi's daughter," he stated firmly, surprised at the pain the idea of never getting close enough to know and acknowledge Rachel as his own caused him.

"But Rafe—" his mother's arm fluttered to her side. The rigid lines of her son's jaw warned her not to pursue the subject.

"I've assured Rafe," Jess broke in, "this is only a passing stop on our way to visit Luke in Venice."

Martha cast a bewildered glance toward Jess. "What?" Then with a firm nod, she added, "Yes. Yes, of course." She took one of the smaller cases hitched under her husband's arm and carried it into the magnificently panelled entry.

Rafe couldn't interpret the emotions on his mother's face as she entered her first love's home. To him she looked strangely serene as her gaze flicked his way. A small sound behind them alerted Rafe to Trudi's presence.

Rafe watched Trudi's approach. No trace of the happy laughing woman before she stepped out of the taxi a few moments earlier remained. The woman confronting them now had armoured her emotions. Rich, golden amber eyes surveyed the three of them.

Rafe set the luggage on the floor and moved toward her. "Trudi, let me introduce my parents, Martha and Jess Hawk."

☙☜☙

In the den, Rafe found the decanter and poured two small whiskies for himself and Jess, and a sherry for his mother.

"We shouldn't have come." Martha turned her distressed gaze to her son.

"No." Rafe sighed. "I wish you'd told me first. I'd have prepared Trudi. Now your visit simply confirms her suspicions that we're in league to take her daughter away from her."

"We'd never do that," Martha responded in amazement. "Who is the other child?" She set her glass down on the coaster protecting the polished surface of the nearby table. "She doesn't resemble her mother."

"Actually," Rafe said, a brief smile lighting his face. "Lizzie is the spitting image of her mother." He perched on the edge of the massive desk on the other side of his mother. "Before her death, Bella and Vince arranged for

Trudi to become Lizzie's legal mother. Lizzie is wonderful about it. She says she's the only child who had two legal moms at the same time."

"It surprised me to learn they'd gone away on holiday so soon after the funeral," his mother stated.

"Another of Bella's pre-arrangements. Apparently, the girls chose the destination. Bella put the plans in place with Trudi's promise to honor them as soon after the funeral as possible. I have to admit, the girls had a wonderful time." He smiled at the memory of their laughter and happiness. "Trudi is an amazing woman," he added softly, before choosing his next words with care.

"You have to remember, she has no recollection of anything that happened the night we escaped from Denny Cadmore's house. Not our flight, the dogs chasing us, the men, or that we jumped into the storm-swollen waters to escape them."

For a moment the girl's excited voices drifted toward them before the click of an outer door closing cut off the sound. Rafe guessed they were headed for the farm and hoped Vince cleared the evidence of the gun battle while they were away.

"There are roughly twenty-four hours to several days she can't account for. And she certainly doesn't remember the rest of the night after we were pulled from the river." Nor did he intend to elaborate on the details now.

"What do you think of the place?" he asked his parents, knowing his mother's curiosity must be eating away at her. He glanced at his step-father. How did Jess feel, being in the home of his wife's first love and the father her first child? The invisible connection between the two men seemed to shimmer in the dust motes dancing in the sunlight.

"We only arrived yesterday. Judy offered to show us around. But after sitting on the plane for hours, we took the opportunity to walk in the grounds and get some exercise." Jess cradled his empty glass in front of him like a shield and studied the prisms of light split by the crystal flute, before looking at his wife. "We better make arrangements to leave."

"But Jess," Martha protested. "We're booked on a flight out in two days."

"Be that as may be." Jess rose from his chair and smiled down at his wife's dismay. "Our presence here will only serve to cause Trudi more distress. If we want to get to know our granddaughter—" He looked at Rafe. "We have to give the girl's mother time to believe in us."

"Thank you, Dad." Rafe clasped Jess's arm.

"What? Now? Right now?" Martha wailed. "This minute? What will Trudi think of us if we leave while she's out?"

"Without meaning to, we've created a situation, dear," Jess said sadly. "We're damned if we do, and we're damned if we don't. I'll phone the airline to reschedule our flight to Venice. If not, you can enjoy a couple of days shopping in London," he promised, smiling at Martha as he pulled out his cell phone.

෬ඁ෬

Trudi pulled out her mobile phone and dialled while the washing machine chugged in the background. Within moments of concluding her call to her solicitor, she collected the girls. With the promise of exploring their new home, the three of them left the Hall to the three Hawks.

No trace of former occupation met Trudi when they entered the farmhouse.

> *We've finished at the farmhouse*, Vince's note, left in her bedroom, had told her. *Don't eat me, but I took advantage of your stay in France and organised a cleaning crew to go through the farmhouse and had someone repair the damage to the walls before you bring the girls here. At the risk of a sharp set-down, I'd like you to contact me if you need any help with the place once you've decided what to do with it.*

Now, as she and the girls examined each room, only the fading smell of pine cleaner permeated the air. Upstairs new glass replaced the shattered window pane, and the two girls bickered playfully over which rooms they wanted until Trudi promised to see if they could build an arch between the rooms to create one big room for them. Whooping with joy, they dashed downstairs and rushed out into the garden.

Trudi opened the window and called down to them. "Stay away from the barns until I join you." Both girls lifted a hand in acknowledgement. Leaning her arm on the window ledge, Trudi watched them rushing around, exploring. Genetically the girls may not be connected, but emotionally their shared bond equalled the strength of most twins.

Only her bond with her own twin had been stronger. Since their argument, that connection had evaporated. No doubt Serena would tell her she deserved the loss.

With a sigh, Trudi closed the window and slowly made her way across the landing. The girls' choice of rooms left Trudi with the one used by the intruder. The knowledge crawled uneasily down her spine. Hastily, she returned to the ground floor, intent on joining the girls, and came face to face with her twin in the open doorway.

Unable to move, Trudi stared at Arthur in bewildered fascination. Had the bond survived after all? Had she sensed his presence without realizing it? She closed her mouth with a snap. Her brother remained still and silent in front of her, watchful, and…?

She tried to identify the emotion flowing from her brother, and with a shock, felt remorse hit her with the velocity of a major explosion. With a cry she opened her arms and flung herself at him.

"What are you doing here? How did you find me? Oh Arthur—" Sobs robbed her ability to continue, and for a moment she gave way to the emotions roiling through her. "The children," she finally managed.

"Serena is with them. They told her you warned them not to enter the barns alone, and they persuaded her to escort them, the little minxes," he said with a laugh. Then he sobered. "Will you let me explain?" he asked her warily.

She nodded. Together they left the house and made their way toward a small bridge stretching across a narrow stream at the end of the grassed area. To Trudi it resembled a hayfield more than a lawn. In unison, they stopped and leaned on the rickety wooden rail and looked down into the clear running water below. Small, gray fish darted from one shadow to the next. A slightly larger one defied the flow, maintaining its rock-steady position in the center of the stream.

"Hindsight is a wonderful thing," Arthur began. "But that's no excuse for the way I bullied you after our parents died."

"But you turned out to be right," she conceded without rancour.

"That's no consolation." He sighed. "In fact it makes it worse."

"How come?" She pulled a protruding splinter of wood from the railing, dropped it into the flow of water below, and ran her finger across the freshness of the exposed surface.

"When our parents died in the plane crash, I wanted to take their place for you and protect you. By doing that, I worked through my grief and lost sight of yours. Instead of being there for you, my actions drove you away. I admit, for a long time, anger compelled me to leave you to your own devices. I persuaded myself you deserved everything you got."

Trudi winced at the echo of Serena's accusations after Bella's funeral.

Arthur continued. "Eventually, when I realized you had sought consolation from Denny because of my actions, I called at his house to find out where you were. He told me the two of you had married, and you'd been killed in an avalanche while skiing during your honeymoon." His eyes swam with unshed tears. "God help me! Trudi, I believed him and stopped searching for you." A kingfisher flashed beneath the bridge where they stood, a sparkle of iridescent blue.

"Sometimes you seemed so close I thought I'd go mad. I tried connecting with you, and the only impression I got was an image of you standing at a window with bars on it. I assumed I was picking up your final emotions while trapped beneath the snow."

Trudi remembered the barren room where she'd spent most of her married life. The small, black, iron-framed bed covered with the meager, worn, gray army blanket, the cracked and pitted mirror on the inside of the wardrobe door hanging drunkenly on its hinges. And the empty fire grate, dull with rust and dust—because Denny refused her the materials to make the room comfortable—and the bare rough floorboards that offered splinters to anyone stupid enough to walk across the floor bare-footed.

And the bars at the window.

She'd spent hours staring at the rooftops between those bars, wondering how she'd ever escape the confines of the room, let alone the house.

Trudi roused herself. "How did you find us now?"

"Rafe heard you leave the house and guessed you'd come here," Arthur said. "His parents were leaving for London, when we arrived."

"What about Rafe?"

"You don't need me to tell you the answer to that one, surely?" Arthur laid a sympathetic hand on her arm. "I'm sorry, Sis. I meant everything for the best. Instead, I've brought you nothing but anguish."

Unable to deny it, she lifted one shoulder and let it drop. "'The road to hell is paved with good intentions,'" she quoted. "Isn't that what they say?" She shifted from watching the fish in the water below to studying her brother's concerned features. "I suppose—" With a grim smile she pointed to the stream. "It's water under the bridge now." Straightening with the intention of joining the girls, she was stopped in her tracks by Arthur's next words.

"The DNA results arrived this morning."

"And?" The impact of his words hit like a nail-bomb finding its target and decimating it, pinning her where she stood.

"He said he won't open it until you return to the Hall, and probably not before the girls are in bed."

"Is that why you're here?" Betrayal buckled her knees, and she grasped the rickety rail to prevent herself from falling. With a contemptuous glance at the barns she targeted her anger at her twin. "Come to gloat? What was it your wife said? Oh yes." She faced her brother. "'I deserve everything I get.' What's she expecting, Arthur? What's she hoping for? That I'll lose everything? My, my. Wouldn't she feel self-righteous?"

Drawing her anger around her like a cloak, Trudi blocked out her twin. Blocked out his news and focussed on her children. Still, fear closed her throat.

With deliberate concentration she released her fingers from their death grip on the railing and headed toward the barns and the sound of their laughter.

The carefree noise brought her to her senses and, slowing down in the middle of the gently swaying grass, she gulped down some long, steadying breaths of air, barely aware Arthur followed close behind her.

Ignoring her outburst, Arthur caught hold of her arm, swung her round to face him folding her in a tight embrace.

"I don't know how," he promised, "but we'll work it out. Together, we'll find the right solution."

In soothing movements his fingers combed through her hair.

CHAPTER 12

R elief washed over Rafe as he emerged from the woods and saw Arthur's arm wrapped protectively around Trudi. From the corner of his vision, he noticed Serena approaching, with the girls close behind her. Changing course, Rafe headed in their direction. The girls ran toward him when he approached, and with one child hanging on each hand, he let them pull him back the way they'd come.

Hearing their happy chatter, Trudi pulled out of her brother's arms and looked over her shoulder in time to spy Rafe ducking his head to follow the girls into one of the dilapidated barns.

"They've discovered a mother cat with five kittens. I don't envy you you're chances of resisting their pleas to keep at least one of them." Laughing, Serena joined them, and together they waited for the cat patrol to return. "Did you enjoy your holiday?"

"Yes. Thank you." Trudi's smile never reached her eyes. "We had a great time." She found it difficult to pretend the easy camaraderie they used to enjoy. "I hope sometime in the not too distant future, I can take them back. They enjoyed themselves so much." She began walking toward the barns. "Time to round up the girls and return to the Hall."

Behind her, Trudi heard the quiet tones of husband and wife. No doubt, Serena was checking up on the outcome of their reunion. The warmth began in her heart and travelled through her whole being at the notion of making peace with her twin. Perhaps she should be grateful to Serena after all. At least her words had given Trudi the incentive to stop looking to others for help.

Admittedly, she'd never considered herself the kind of woman who depended on others to get her out of a fix. She paused outside the barn door that was desperately clinging to one hinge. Did Serena's opinion matter? Trudi asked herself then dipped her head before entering building.

Taking a moment to adjust her eyes to the dimness inside, she focussed on the three figures squatting in the straw a few feet in front of her. Dust motes danced in a stray sunbeam that landed at her feet. Rachel knelt on the straw littered floor. Lizzie sat crossed legged next to her. Hunkered back on his heels with his jacket slung over his shoulder, Rafe bent his head close to Rachel's while they focussed on the tiny mewing kitten in the palm of his hand. The mother cat, lying in a nest of straw in front of them, watched the intruders with amazing tolerance and trust, Trudi thought, her lips curving in a gentle smile.

Whether he sensed her presence or heard her approach, she didn't know, but the warmth of Rafe's smile set her pulse thrumming. Her heart danced at the sight of it, and her hands ached to touch him. Her breasts swelled, and her nipples hardened under his surveillance. Aware of the warmth stealing up her neck and into her face, she shifted her gaze to her daughter's radiant expression.

"Mum," Rachel whispered, "come and look at these kittens." She shifted to make a space for Trudi beside Rafe. "We've called the mother cat Marmalade."

"It's the first time I've seen a ginger female cat," Rafe said quietly. "Someone told me ginger cats were tomcats."

"How many kittens does she have?" Careful not to alarm the feline parent, Trudi settled herself on the floor.

"Five." Lizzie held up a pale marmalade colored kitten next to the black one now asleep in Rafe's hand. "There's a black, a white, a ginger, and two gray kittens."

"Can we keep one?" Rachel pleaded.

"Well, they're still too young to leave their mother," Trudi said. "Let's wait until we move before we make any decisions."

"Move?" Rafe demanded, forgetting to keep his voice low.

Alarmed the mother cat nudged his hand with her nose. Rafe gently returned her kitten to the nest of straw.

Catching Trudi's arm with one hand, he drew her up with him and moved away from the children.

"What do you mean, move?" he asked again.

"Let go of my arm," Trudi hissed, trying to pull her arm out of his grip.

"Not until you answer my question," Rafe returned, his gray eyes darkening like knapped flint. "I came to tell you the DNA results have arrived."

Pulling once more on her arm, Trudi tried to control her panic. "Arthur told me. When are you going to reveal the results?"

"When the girls are in bed, and we have time to ourselves to talk things through. And we can't if you spirit the girls away without notice."

"Don't be absurd, Rafe." She strove for a tone of indifference she was far from feeling. "Since Bella left the farm to me, it makes sense for us to make it our home. I'm hardly spiriting them away."

"What about the Hall?" A shaft of sunlight caught and emphasized the sharp angles of his face, revealing the shock reflected in his eyes.

"What about it?" Trudi shot back.

"You inherited it. What will you do with it when you move out? What about Judy and the Frobishers? What will happen to them?"

"Nothing," Trudi replied in surprise. "Vince's department has a contract which means my presence won't affect them one iota."

"Explain," Rafe snapped.

"I beg your pardon?"

If he wasn't so annoyed, Rafe would have laughed at her regal tone. "The first day I arrived, you said you inherited Kinsale Hall from your husband."

"I also said I didn't want anything to do with the place," Trudi snapped right back at him.

"Why did you?" Rafe demanded.

Her shoulders slumped at the invading memories. "They said I deserved the place."

"Who did? Why would they say that?"

"Vince and Arthur said if I accepted the solicitors' demands, Bella and I would have a secure future."

"So you agreed?" Rafe asked flatly, unable to explain the disappointment plaguing him.

"No. I didn't." Trudi shifted her weight from one foot to the other, her arms curled around her waist.

"What persuaded you to accept the inheritance?" Rafe leaned his shoulder against the wooden ladder leading to the loft.

A quick glance toward the girls reassured Trudi they were still focussed on the mother cat and her kittens.

"Vince commissioned the place as a Safe House for his returning agents."

"Go on." He rubbed his shoulder against the ladder to relieve an itch.

"I agreed, on condition the solicitors return the Hall to the rightful owners when and if they are ever found." Trudi sent a challenging stare in his direction.

A chill of apprehension shivered down his spine. Did Trudi suspect?

"Surely as your husband's widow you are the rightful heir?" He asked in a carefully controlled tone.

"According to the solicitors, Denny wasn't the rightful heir. But because they couldn't trace the legal heir, they declared him missing, presumed dead, and allowed Denny to inherit."

"Why did you call yourself the caretaker, when we met?"

"I've explained why."

Exasperated, Trudi began moving toward the girls. Rafe moved so fast, one moment he leaned against the ladder, the next he'd blocked her path to the children.

"No," he said. "Why do you say your tenure at the Hall isn't valid?"

"I can't explain it." Trudi sighed. "My gut tells me the rightful owner is not dead. I don't even believe he's missing."

Rafe combed his fingers through his hair, half turned to glance out through the open doorway and back at her. His smoky gray eyes smouldered with emotion.

"Why would you think that?" he burst out. "When, by your own words, you say the solicitors can't trace him? That's lunacy."

"Perhaps," she replied calmly. The more bothered Rafe appeared the more composed Trudi became.

"It doesn't make sense," he muttered.

"I've already said so."

Without knowing why, Trudi gained a perverse sense of pleasure from witnessing his angst. Perhaps because he'd always displayed a cool control in adversity until now. But it still didn't explain his reaction to her comments.

"We seem to have strayed from the point," she reminded him. "We are moving to the farm. It will be better for the girls. Lizzie knows this place belonged to her mum, and she's more than happy to leave the Hall. Rachel can't wait to restore the barns and convert part of one into a full-blown playroom where they can have their own private space."

"When do you plan to put this into action?" Rafe asked.

"I've already instructed the solicitors to deal directly with Vince in future. As for moving to the farm, we'll move when I've gathered enough furniture to make the house habitable for us."

"There a lot of furniture going to waste at the Hall. Have you considered using some of it?"

"I considered it." Trudi looked up at his serious expression. "But none of it's mine, nor would it be right at the farm."

"You've been through the furniture in the closed wing of the Hall?"

"Of course not," Trudi sputtered. "Why are you making such an issue about this?"

"You seem to have forgotten about the test results waiting for our perusal later this evening. We both know it's simply a formality, unless—" Rafe paused deliberately,

"You slept with every man you met during the period your memory let you down."

Guilt rocked through him at the sight of her chalk-white face. The need to penetrate her air of independence clawed at him. The vision of Trudi walking away with the girls regardless of the DNA tests haunted him. Her intention to move them out of the Hall magnified his fears.

"Once again, you make your opinion of me quite clear. It's a constant source of amazement to me you stick around, unless—" Mimicking his actions, she paused. "You intend to file for custody. Or are you intending to go for plain and simple abduction? Is that why your parent's turned up? Were they checking in to confirm your plans fit together?

"Are they even now waiting at the airport for you to take Rachel to them? A child with an elderly couple would not be stopped if the police believed they were looking for a father-daughter combination, would they?" Trudi hissed.

Turning to the girls, she called them over. After a little fuss on their part, together they left the barn.

Heading for the path back to the Hall, Trudi wondered why she loved the wretched man. Loved? Ridiculous. She'd vowed never to trust her heart to another man again. Love had nothing to do with her feelings. Fascination, definitely, lust possibly, but love?

Never in a million years!

෴

After the sound of their footsteps faded, Rafe left the barn to discover Arthur standing on the narrow bridge. The outcome of the DNA tests would have the same effect on him as on Trudi, Rafe realized suddenly. The rising dew topping each blade of grass beneath his feet went unnoticed.

"Have you told her?" Arthur's face angled toward him, half in fading sunlight the rest in shadow, hiding his eyes from Rafe's gaze.

Rafe leaned on the rail in a parody of Trudi's recent position. "I suggested we wait and open it together when the girls are in bed."

"That seems reasonable," Arthur replied artlessly. "What else did you do to put her in a snit again?" he added, turning his hard gaze toward his companion.

"Did she tell you she intends to move into the farm immediately?" Rafe asked.

"No, but it doesn't surprise me," Arthur admitted.

"Why?" Rafe's hand crashed down on the rail.

"She never wanted the Hall. Vince persuaded her to take it on."

"I find it hard to believe anyone could persuade Trudi to do something she didn't want to," Rafe snapped.

Arthur laughed. "Vince used Bella."

"Used Bella?" Rafe repeated, shaking his head in confusion. "How?"

"You have to understand both women were in abusive relationships. Vince promised them safety and security if Trudi accepted the inheritance. He wanted somewhere safe for his sister and our agents and other people who needed security and a place of safety for a while. Judy and the Frobishers are permanent residents who look after any of our people when they arrive. To outsiders, they are residents in an exclusive seniors' accommodation."

Rafe stared at Arthur. "But as Cadmore's widow Trudi's legally entitled to the inheritance."

"Come off it, Rafe," Arthur snapped back. "We both know the truth. If you think she won't find out, you're a fool. And God help you when she does."

When Arthur started walking toward the woods, Rafe followed. He'd known Arthur long enough to know his friend hadn't finished speaking.

"Out with it, man." Rafe fell into step with Arthur as they approached the edge of the woods.

"What are your intentions toward my sister?" he asked.

"If the tests confirm I'm Rachel's father, it makes sense for Trudi to marry me." Rafe watched surprise followed by anger settle on his companion's face.

"Not in my lifetime, she won't." Arthur grabbed Rafe's arm, preventing him from moving off. His slim build belied his strength. "She's been the victim of one bad marriage. I won't allow you to trap her in a second."

"Given you're responsible for bringing us together, I find that rich," Rafe snorted. *Why would Trudi feel trapped?* Disbelief warred with rage at Arthur's words. For minutes, the ability to respond failed him. The blood pulsed in his ears. "She wouldn't be trapped," he shouted.

"Of course she would."

Arthur's finger prodding his chest almost provoked Rafe into hitting the chin precariously close to his own face.

"Damn it man, I'd never trap her into marriage. I love the woman."

An eerie silence settled among the surrounding trees as Rafe's words echoed in his brain. He watched Arthur's mouth form a startled O before turning into a full-blown grin.

"Well, why didn't you say so?" he asked, his vise-like grip pumping Rafe's hand up and down. "Have you told her?" Arthur's smile faded.

"No." Rafe raked his fingers through his honey-blond hair, and began walking again without waiting for Arthur. "How can I?" he added, almost too quietly for Arthur to catch. "When I raised the subject before, she accused me of trying to manipulate her to get closer to Rachel."

"She said that?" Arthur asked in shocked tones.

"Not in so many words," Rafe admitted. "But her meaning was clear enough."

When they reached the clearing where he'd observed Trudi watching the fawn, he headed for the log and sat down. Arthur joined him, sitting almost exactly where his sister sat on the day of Bella's funeral.

"When the first people we saw on arrival home were my parents, everything Trudi and I shared in France evaporated," Rafe said. "She doesn't trust me. Thinks my parents and I are in collusion to spirit Rachel away from her. The hell of it is, I understand her fear. The same way I understand my parent's pain."

"I don't understand." Arthur picked up a leaf and skewered it on a protruding spine from the log. "About your parents, I mean."

"If—no, when I marry your sister, my full name has to be registered. Hopefully, Megan and Luke will both attend. The only surprise is, Megan hasn't made the connection between Kinsale Hall and Rafael Kinsale Hawk," Rafe explained. "I mean—" Rafe paused again. "Kinsale is not a common name."

Stunned, Arthur turned from his contemplation of the tattered leaf to study his companion. "Are you telling me your brother and sister don't realize Jess is not your birth father?"

"Exactly." Rafe twisted from studying the ground beneath his feet to staring at his friend. "My mother wants me to try and keep the information quiet. But how can I? Even if Megan doesn't work it out, Luke certainly will. And he won't hesitate to bring up the question openly.

"Like Daniel Kinsale before me, I have to choose between my parents and family, or the woman I love, my daughter and Lizzie. Trudi and the girls win hands down. That's where Daniel Kinsale and I differ. But the thought of hurting my family in the process, is the pits. And—"

Deep lines furrowed his brow. "Trudi told me in the barn, she's convinced the true heir to the Hall is still alive, and she's instructed the solicitors to start looking for him again." He watched Arthur quietly observing him. "Note her use of 'him.' Is she psychic or something?"

"She had an uncanny ability for being right more often than I liked when we were children," Arthur responded in a wry tone.

"She's already convinced herself I suggested marriage to ensure my place in Rachel's life. If she discovers my entitlement to Kinsale Hall, I won't stand a snowball's chance in Hell with her." Rafe groaned. "She'll never believe I won't try to take Rachel away from her."

"Don't under estimate my sister," Arthur suggested in a firm voice. "Come on. If nothing else, Serena will have my hide if I'm late."

"You're going somewhere?" Rafe asked, his mind still focussed on Trudi's reception when they arrived back at the Hall.

"No. She offered to cook tonight, and she hates when people are late for her meals." Arthur shoved off the log and headed toward the Hall.

�

Illusions. Nothing but illusions. Trudi berated herself for daring to dream. To hope things might be different between her and Rafe.

She couldn't say when her fear and resentment changed toward Rafe. The memory of the afternoon she watched the fawn, and he'd cradled her in his arms, came to mind. The shared laughter during their trip to Disney and the days spent in Paris. Contrary to all her expectations, he'd proved a wonderful, witty, and charming companion when he'd appeared at their apartment door at Disneyland and during the following days.

The rightness of the happy unit they'd become for those few days—were those feelings an illusion?

Reality in the shape of his parents standing on the steps of Kinsale Hall had shattered her developing dreams, replacing them with uncertainty.

"Mum, are you ready yet?" Rachel bounced into her room.

"Nearly, love. Why don't you and Lizzie go down and tell Aunt Serena I'll follow shortly?"

"Okay." Rachel gave her a quick bear-hug and dashed from the room.

Their footsteps faded as they charged for the stairs, followed by silence and a thud. The banister, it seemed, was still the fastest route to the bottom of the stairs. Trudi's lips curved in a fond smile. She leaned forward, added a touch of lip-gloss, then hesitated. If the DNA result confirmed Rafe's parentage, everything in her life, and Rachel's, changed forever tonight. Rachel would no longer be "her" daughter, but "their" daughter. To assume Rafe accepted the status quo meant living in a fool's paradise. It wouldn't work.

A shiver skittered down her spine. She imagined Rafe's arms around her, his lips caressing her, his love engulfing—Stop, she ordered herself. He'd suggested marriage to secure a place in his daughter's life. The idea of entering another sham marriage horrified her. A marriage couldn't be built on the spark of electricity crackling between them when they touched. Lust never lasted.

Rafe's arrival at the Hall had reawakened emotions in Trudi she'd long since assumed had atrophied and died. Emotions unwanted in the safe world she'd built for herself, Bella, and the girls. Now, at the sound of his voice, her whole body quivered with anticipation. Her dreams went into overdrive, and her common sense took a nosedive. And tonight everything she'd striven for would turn to ashes. Once the results were known, her hard won independence would evaporate. Somehow they must reach an agreement before they told the children. *And what about Rachel's rights?* a small internal voice prompted.

Though she may not have told the whole truth, Trudi had never lied to her daughter when she'd asked about her father. Not knowing the whereabouts of her father became the reality Rachel grew up with. Trudi didn't like it, but she hadn't known how else to answer Rachel the first time the question arose.

With a sigh, Trudi acknowledged time ran out for her the day Rafe walked back into her life. She may not remember the night he claimed they made love, but surely no man in his right mind would try to claim parentage of a child he hadn't conceived. And Rafe seemed eager to accept the responsibilities of parenthood. Therein lay the heart of her problem. For the sake of the girls, Trudi accepted she'd consider most options between her and Rafe. But marriage? Impossible.

Bound to someone who tolerated her simply to get close to his child would destroy her as much, perhaps more, devastatingly than her marriage to Denny. With him, her illusions of love had died within hours of the ink drying on the certificate. With Rafe, love didn't enter the equation, simply cold-blooded expediency. One-sided love never worked. She'd loved Denny to distraction, and it hadn't taken him long to destroy it.

Trudi ran the brush through her hair, dropped it back on the surface, spun away from her reflection, and headed downstairs.

CHAPTER 13

R afe wanted Arthur and Serena gone. The meal had been simple and delicious. The girls relived their holiday experiences for their aunt and uncle before wilting and reluctantly going to bed. And still the couple stayed. He glanced in Trudi's direction and recognized the same tension in her face that gripped him.

"Which room has Judy given you?" He smiled at Serena.

"Oh we're not staying." Her surprise evident, Serena looked at her watch and then at Arthur, exclaiming, "Oh my. Look at the time. We'd better be going. Otherwise our babysitter will quit on us. We promised not to be late home," she added. Reluctantly, she rose from her chair, waiting for her husband to follow.

With an amused glance in Rafe's direction, Trudi jumped up to collect their coats and Serena's bag from the rack in the panelled hall.

"Quite," Arthur agreed with his wife. "Cheryl has exams next week. Won't do to interrupt her study time." His mouth lifted at one corner.

Hard put to refrain from bursting into full-throated laughter at his friend's pompous attempt to cover his interest in the DNA results, Rafe took the coat Trudi passed him and held it for Serena to slip her arms into. Taking pity on her, Rafe drew Serena ahead of the others.

"It's better if we open the results alone," he said softly. "I know you understand."

"Of course." Serena squeezed his arm in return.

"Arthur?"

With a wry grin, Rafe watched Serena hesitate when she realized brother and sister were deep in conversation and hadn't heard her approach. He sighed when Trudi pulled away from the hand resting on her shoulder.

"Come on Arthur," Serena said. "We've overstayed our welcome. Time to give these two the privacy they need. They'll keep us informed when they're ready."

Rafe choked back a laugh when Trudi cast a wide-eyed look of surprise at her sister-in-law's understanding glance. Then he sobered at the sight of the dark stain of embarrassment creeping up Serena's neck. She moved to her husband's side and laid a persuasive hand on his elbow.

"Come," she encouraged quietly, and guided him towards the open front door.

ℰℐℰℐ

In silence, Trudi stood beside Rafe at the top of the steps and watched the red tail lights fade into the distance. The warmth of his arm resting on her shoulders felt both comforting and restricting at the same time. Confusion, followed by fear, swept through her. Anxious as she'd been to see her brother and his wife leave, now she almost wished they'd stayed longer.

Regardless of the contents of the manila envelope resting on her desk top, her life would change forever. And she didn't know if she could cope with another change.

"Don't be afraid, Trudi." She looked up when Rafe's soft words penetrated her fear. "Whatever the results, we'll work through them together," he said. "No pressure, no expectations."

No expectations? Of course, he had expectations. He wanted to get close to his daughter.

What of her expectations? She expected him to make demands she didn't want to contemplate, like flying Rachel to The States to stay with his family. Fear of losing Rachel to her American relatives, and the impact on Lizzie, almost buckled her knees.

"I am afraid, Rafe." Shock held her rigid. Had she admitted her fears aloud?

"Of course, you are," Rafe agreed. "I understand. But we have to work through this together for the sake of the girls." His thumb brushed the back of her hand and warmth spread up her wrist and arm and pierced her heart. "And we owe it to ourselves."

"No pressure?" Trudi looked into the smoky-gray eyes holding her gaze and watched them darken with emotion.

"No pressure," he agreed firmly. "Come," he said, unwittingly parodying Serena's command to her brother.

Trudi followed him into the house and stood quietly beside him while Rafe closed and bolted the heavy wooden-panelled door. Together, still with his arm circling her waist, they headed for the study.

"A drink?" Rafe asked.

Trudi nodded and made for the wing chair beside the desk. From there she watched Rafe pour a small measure of amber liquid into two glasses and hand one to her.

She nodded again and waited until he sat down with the envelope resting in his lap and took a sip from his glass.

"Are you ready?"

Trudi shook her head and smiled. "No, but open it anyway."

The sound of the paper knife slicing through the sealed flap filled the silence, followed by the swish of paper being withdrawn.

ↄ/ↄ

"The test is positive." Rafe passed the single sheet to Trudi. "This confirms I'm Rachel's father."

Confirmation of the suspected truth filled him with awe. His daughter! He had a child, not just any child but one he already loved and took pride in. Unaware of his falling tears, Rafe stared at Trudi.

"I have a daughter," he whispered. "A beautiful daughter."

Her fingertips brushed the tears from his eyes, and he realised she'd moved to sit on his lap. One arm laid comfortingly around the back of his shoulder, the other, a mother's touch, caressed his cheek. Her eyes dark with emotion he could only guess at, she gave herself to him sweetly, unhesitatingly, sharing his joy of being a father. He pulled her face close to his and kissed her firmly on the mouth.

The DNA results fluttered to the floor when his hands wrapped around her slender body, pulling her close until the soft swell of her breasts crushed against the firm wall of his chest. The mother of his child was in his arms once more, and he felt complete. He experienced a sense of homecoming.

Her scent filled him, a mixture of soap and fresh flowers, setting his pulse on fire. His hands caressed down her back and slipped beneath her floral print cotton shirt. Her warm skin rippled beneath his fingers.

Like a skittish colt, her flesh welcomed his touch while the owner was ready to flee. He teased her lips open with his tongue and gave her no chance to retreat. Their tongues danced to a tune of their own making. Trudi moved on his lap, allowing his hand to creep round to cup her breast.

The sound of her low-throated moan when he flicked his thumb across the tip of her hardened nipple drove him on. With the other hand he released her lacy slip of a bra and pushed her shirt up exposing the creamy swell of her breasts. His head dipped, and his lips paid homage, first to one and then the other. He opened his eyes to see her head flung back, her eyes closed and an expression of wonderment on her face. He wanted to take her upstairs, to share the experience of true fulfilment with her.

❡❦❡

Trudi's fingers released the buttons on his shirt exposing the golden tan of his muscled chest. The touch of his lips on hers encouraged, welcomed, *demanded* a response from her. Tongue twisting with tongue and dancing together shot passions she'd never known coursing through her, heating her, driving her on to match him. His hands on her skin drove her mad with a wanting she didn't understand.

Instinctively, her fingers found and released the rest of his shirt buttons, her hands sweeping the width of his powerful torso. Her lips wanted to follow but were unable to, due to Rafe's tongue teasing her nipples. A soul-deep throbbing between her legs drove her on. For the first time in her life she felt beautiful and thrust herself forward eager for his touch, eager to touch him, but unsure of his expectations.

The cool air on her skin brought her back to reality. She opened her eyes to see Rafe's brow resting against her breasts.

"Rafe?"

He looked up, sadness filling his eyes. "This is wrong," he said quietly, pulling her shirt closed.

Mortified, she slipped off his lap and turned her back on him while she straightened her clothes. She bent down to retrieve the sheet of paper he'd dropped earlier. The blood drained from her face as she stared at the words above the results.

"Trudi, you are beautiful. Under other circumstance I'd have taken you to bed by now." Rafe's voice shook with emotion. His words faltered. "I—I want you like I've never wanted a woman before, but now is not the time."

Alerted by her sudden stillness, he moved to look at her face. Shock and betrayal reflected back at him.

"What is it?"

Rafe reached out for her. She twisted away from his seeking hands and glared at him, her mouth working, but unable to get the words out into the open. The paper still in her hand, she crossed to her chair picked up her glass and flung the contents in his face.

"How could you?"

Her features contorted, she flung the empty glass at him, striking him on the cheek.

The sound of the glass shattering on the floor released Rafe from his shocked stance.

"I tell you how beautiful you are, and this is your response?" he roared. "No wondered Cadmore went elsewhere for his pleasure."

"I'm not the one called Kinsale, so don't try making me the villain here," she shrieked in return, waving the sheet of paper in his face. "Rafe Kinsale Hawk."

She wrapped her arms around her waist and swung away before spinning back to face him. All trace of emotion stripped from her face, her voice flat and lifeless.

"You were careful to keep that dirty little secret under wraps, weren't you? Apparently, you don't sign your full name on your work contracts." She studied him. "Or do you?" She paused. "And this afternoon? When I told you how I believed the rightful heir not only lived—" Trudi took a deep breath. "But wilfully refused to claim his inheritance, you still said nothing. You hypocritical bastard!"

Rafe saw the small gleam of satisfaction flood her eyes when he flinched at her accusation, but it didn't last.

"Get out. Get out now and never come back."

The sound of her cold flat tone filled Rafe's soul with fear.

"You can't deny the results of the tests."

"I don't give a damn about the tests. You're a liar and a cheat." She held her hand up before he could respond. "You lied by omission and cheated your way into my daughter's life in an attempt to get a foothold in her affection, once you were faced with having to take this test."

Again she shook the paper in the air. "Go back to your family and tell them…" She ran out of words, tears choking her throat.

"Tell them what Trudi? That their granddaughter's mother is denying them access to her?" he snarled. "And what will you tell Rachel?"

"What will you tell me, Mummy?" Rachel's sleep filled voice echoed from the open doorway.

Shocked silence filled the room. The adults first stared at each other and then at their daughter standing silhouetted by the light flooding in from the hall.

❧❧❧

"Can't you sleep, darling?"

Trudi rushed across the room and engulfed her daughter in a fierce hug. Across the top of Rachel's head she shot a furious glance at Rafe.

"I heard you shouting and thought you were having a nightmare. When I didn't find you in your room I came looking for you," she explained.

"Do you have many nightmares?"

The concern in Rafe's voice almost undid her. Holding onto her anger, she faced him.

"Don't we all?" she countered.

"What were you going to tell me?" Rachel repeated, looking from her mother to the father she didn't realise she had.

"Rafe is leaving," Trudi stated firmly, watching anger darken his eyes.

"Will he come back?" Rachel studied her mother's tight features.

"You better believe it, pumpkin," Rafe muttered.

"I'm not a pumpkin." Rachel laughed, before flinging herself at Rafe. "You'll come back soon, won't you?"

"You better believe it," he promised again, his dark gaze fastening on Trudi. "Go back to bed, hon. I want a quick word with your mom before she tucks you in again."

Dropping on one knee, Rafe hugged his child, brushed a quick kiss across her forehead before standing and releasing her.

"Night, Rafe." she said. "Come back soon." Rachel disappeared back the way she'd come.

Moving swiftly, Rafe grasped Trudi's wrist firmly and thrust his face towards hers. "Just because I didn't say anything tonight doesn't mean I won't," he said, his furious tone cold and low. "I spoke the truth when I told my daughter—" He paused as pain flitted across Trudi's face. "I'll be back when I've sorted my business commitments, and I expect you to be here when I return."

"Not in a million years," Trudi snapped. "I've looked after your place long enough. We move to the farm by the end of the week. If you try to harass me or my children—" Imitating Rafe, Trudi paused to let her words sink in. "I will instigate legal proceedings against you. I'll never become a victim of intimidation ever again," she added before walking round him and leaving the room.

ഇൻഇ

She couldn't have wounded him more deliberately if she'd tried, he acknowledged in the ensuing silence. With a sigh Rafe accepted they'd come full circle. Her threat of harassment charges proved that. Briefly, he searched for the sheet with the DNA results before realizing Trudi still had it when she left.

His brief euphoria evaporated. Swallowing the last of his whiskey, Rafe thumped his tumbler on the desk and stepped round the shards of glass still on the floor. Fetching a brush and pan from the kitchen, he cleared the debris away before heading upstairs to pack his bags.

An hour later, secure in the knowledge Trudi couldn't possibly manage to move into the farm before he returned, Rafe pulled out his cell phone and dialled for a taxi.

ഇൻഇ

Terrified Rafe would return sooner than anticipated, Trudi spent the following days searching the shops for furniture, coaxing retailers to make special deliveries, and working every spare moment she had to get the farm ready for them to move in by the end of the week.

Judy gave up trying to dissuade her and agreed to listen for the girls at night, allowing Trudi to work at the farm. One day she hit the do-it-yourself stores and returned with tins of paint, brushes, wallpaper, glue, and other paraphernalia needed to get the place ready. She worked solidly through the day, returning when the children arrived back from school, and retracing her steps after the girls were in bed.

She lost weight. Her eyes dulled and merged with the surrounding dark smudges. Not one brush stroke of paint, or the fixing of loose door hinges, or the scrubbing of floors drove from her mind the memory of Rafe's face when she'd discovered his identity.

Nothing she did filled the emptiness his betrayal created. Almost—almost, she'd believed they had a chance together. Her skin tingled at the memory of his touch. Under the darkness of night, her bed seemed unbearably empty. She didn't understand how, since she'd slept alone for most of her life. Even to Denny, she'd been nothing more than a handy relief.

She woke in the night, pulsating with need for Rafe. A need he'd awakened in her. How she damned him for that! When she slept, the covers tangled into a crumpled mass on the floor from her tossing and turning. She rose in the mornings, feeling more tired than ever.

She dreamed of his arms around her only to watch him walk away and hear Denny laughing at her. '*You're not loveable.*'

The cruel words woke her from her nightmares, and grateful for the interruption, she dressed, left a note for Judy, and headed back in the darkness to work some more at the farm, before returning in time to give the girls their breakfast and see them off to school.

"You're killing yourself," Judy remonstrated with her on Friday morning after the girls left.

"It's nearly done," Trudi lied. "I want to move our stuff out of here and into the farm before they get home this afternoon."

❧❧❧

"Have you told them you're moving them so quickly?" Judy asked.

She didn't know the details, but word of Rafe's true identity had filtered down to Vince's agents. And Trudi refused to explain her hasty departure from Kinsale Hall.

"Of course I have." Trudi's aggrieved tone startled Judy.

"At least let me help you," Judy insisted. She huffed when Trudi shook her head.

"You're not here to help me. You're part of Vince's staff, not mine."

"Undeniable, but that doesn't stop me wanting to help a friend." Judy took the bundle of clothes Trudi held and placed them in the cardboard box on the bed. "I'll collect and pack Lizzie's stuff while you clear Rachel's room." She gave Trudi a gentle shove in the direction of chest of drawers.

By midday they'd cleared both rooms, transferred the contents to the farmhouse, and put them away in the cupboards and drawers Trudi bought at the start of the week. The smell of paint was fading. The brightly colored rooms looked cheerful and welcoming—pinks and different shades of pale orange and yellow for Rachel, blues and shades of sea green for Lizzie.

A portrait of Bella hung on the wall at the end of Lizzie's bed. The small, gold-guilt clock Bella loved sat on the bedside table. A rich-textured rug covered the polished wooden floor, and Lizzie's favourite dolls snuggled together on a comfy chair near a window framed with silver gray curtains with a hint of green that matched the decor.

When Judy finished in Lizzie's room, she found Trudi still adding the final items to Rachel's chest of drawers. She'd painted the cupboards in here a deep dusky pink that matched the curtains. The bedspread ranged from a pale orange at one end to a rich pink at the other. Surprised the colors blended so well, she noticed the tiny easel Trudi placed in the corner of the room. Judy smiled. On the dividing wall between the two rooms Trudi had painted an open arched doorway, indicating where, in time, she planned to create an aperture to connect the two rooms.

Leaving Trudi to finish up in Rachel's room, Judy strolled into the final bedroom and gasped. Strips of dark and dirty paper peeled off the walls. The bare floorboards, twisted and cracked, creating a hazard for the unwary occupant in the dark. The light flex from the ceiling ended with a single, un-shaded bulb. The narrow black-painted iron bed frame stood in bits against the far wall, along with a mattress. She cursed under her breath at her friend's stubbornness, while appreciating the care and work the mother had put in for her children.

The sound of someone climbing the stairs drew her out of the room. She nearly choked at the sight of Rafe's angry face immediately in front of her.

"Where is she?" he demanded.

Silently Judy pointed to Rachel's room, then moved round him and hastened downstairs to the kitchen for cleaning materials.

∽∾∽

Shaking with rage, Rafe stood in the bedroom doorway and watched Trudi fill the last drawer with Rachel's clothes. Arriving at the Hall to discover she'd made good on her promise to move out filled him with fear and anger in equal parts. Now watching her slow deliberate movements the anger evaporated, leaving the fear gnawing at his gut.

She looked like a zombie. Her shoulders stooped. Her hair resembled a crow's nest. Mismatched socks were on her feet. And when she looked in his direction with eyes glazed from lack of sleep, he couldn't decide whether to kiss his stubborn darling or rant and rage at her.

"What can I do to help?" he asked, startling them both.

Closing the gap between them, he took the pile of clothes from Trudi's nerveless fingers and began placing them carefully in the open drawer. The bed springs squeaked behind him. In the mirror, he saw her gaping at him, too tired to take in the turn of events. He fully intended to make the most of it. With a snap he closed the drawer.

He studied Trudi's reflection, waiting until she raised her eyes to meet his gaze. "I'm here for the long-haul." His soft words hung in the silence. Her gaze never wavered from his reflection. "I'm moving my headquarters here. My staff will be joining me in a couple of weeks and staying until I can find British replacements." Still, Trudi's owl-like stare held steady. Rafe stared right back.

"I intend to be a part of Rachel's life. Get used to it." Shoving himself away from the chest of drawers, Rafe stuffed his fists into his pockets, crossed the floor, and bent towards her. "Tell me what the next job is?" he asked quietly, and taking one of her hands in his, he pulled her off the bed and enfolded her in his arms.

For a moment she leaned into him and rested her cheek against his chest. He caressed her hair with one hand and rested his chin on top of her head.

"I won't deny I'd prefer us under the same roof. But I accept your need to move the girls here. So let's get on with it before they get home from school." With a gentle push he released her and moved towards the door.

"Rafe?" Fatigue slowed her movements. "Thank you." She pushed a strand of hair away from her face, a frown creasing her brow.

"What's the matter?" His hand on the knob he stopped when Trudi didn't moved.

"I'm trying to think." Her voice was thick and slurred. "The kitchen, I forgot to bring the stuff I bought for the kitchen."

"Tell me where it is, and I'll fetch it over. First if you have a kettle, let's have a coffee before we do any more."

Rafe took Trudi's hand and led the way to the kitchen. Gently, he pushed her into a chair and set about filling the kettle from the tap. He raided the cupboard until he found two mugs, remembered Judy and collected another. Soon the scent of coffee filled the room. Trudi liked hers strong with a little milk, and after a brief search he discovered the milk in the walk-in pantry.

"Where's your fridge?"

Surprise crossed Trudi's face when she looked round. "I haven't got one."

Concerned, Rafe wondered if she remembered how she'd got here.

"When is it coming?" he asked, assuming she'd ordered one.

"Not yet." Trudi wrapped her hands around her mug.

Without a word, Rafe picked up the third mug and left the kitchen. Sounds from the living room led him to Judy, industriously clearing the dust from the windowsill.

"I've brought you a coffee," he said.

"Thank you." A smile crinkled the laugh lines around her eyes then faded. Silently she sipped her coffee, her gaze never leaving his face.

"What?" Rafe asked, knowing the older woman was weighing her words.

"I haven't known Trudi long." Judy hesitated. "And I don't have her full history, only what Vince deemed necessary for me as her minder. I've seen enough to know she's on the edge of a breakdown. To look at her you might assume she's suffering from physical tiredness, and without a doubt that's true. But beneath the façade, it's grief that's eating away at her.

"Grief doesn't wait for friends to pass before it hits. Trudi's been in a state of grief for many months, knowing nothing could save Bella. In that time she's been there for her friend and the children. The scare of the intruder meant the girls' safety presented an added burden. Not that Trudi saw it as such. You mean well, but your presence is pushing her reserves into the danger zone.

"All her beliefs have been shaken in the past few weeks, her trust shattered. Only her personal strength is sustaining her now." Judy lifted her mug to her lips, her eyes watchful over the rim.

"I hear what you're saying. I've told Trudi, and I'll tell you. I'm moving my business headquarters from Boston to the U.K., and am here for however long it takes."

"Does Vince know?" Judy couldn't hide her surprise.

"Vince is aware of the changed situation, and we'll be discussing the future shortly." Rafe's clipped tone didn't invite further questions.

Silently Judy handed her empty mug back to him. "I'll finish here and go back to the Hall to see to the girls. They'll be delighted to learn you've returned."

"Thank you." Rafe's smile lit up his face, his smoky eyes turning a silvery-gray. "Can you advise me where I might get a fridge and freezer delivered immediately?"

Judy passed on the required information before stepping forward and placing a detaining hand on his arm.

"I suggest you take another look upstairs," she offered quietly before resuming her cleaning.

Puzzled, Rafe took the stairs two at a time. Heading first to Lizzie's room and finding it ready to receive its new occupant, he moved swiftly across the landing to the last bedroom. A startled hiss whistled through tight lips when he studied the dilapidation.

Crossing the room, he pulled on a piece of peeling wall paper and watched the dust follow the paper to the floor. The mattress leaning against the wall and the old blanket folded neatly along the top had seen better days. Faced with the evidence of her determination to get away from the hall before his return, guilt swept through him.

He banged his fist on the mattress, and choked when a cloud of dust flew into the air. He strode from the room and headed for the kitchen. His target was fast asleep where he'd left her, her unfinished coffee cooling beside her.

CHAPTER 14

He'd come back. Trudi woke to sun spilling through the window, the mantra still running through her mind. He'd come back. She snuggled into the warmth of the duvet savouring the fresh sharp smell of cologne. *Cologne?*

Her eyes flew open and immediately focused on Rafe's silhouette at the window. Had she made some sound, she wondered, when Rafe gave her a wary smile.

"Feeling better?" He moved to sit on the edge of her bed.

She nodded wordlessly, wondering when and how the bed had arrived at the farmhouse, and who'd put her to bed. Nervously her hand tunnelled beneath the duvet and discovered her old comfortable t-shirt.

"Judy." Rafe answered the silent question in her eyes.

"Oh. Thank you. What time is it? Where are the girls?" she added.

"Three fifteen."

Even after the work she'd put in over the past few days, she couldn't believe she slept for so long. Her initial shock increased when Rafe's grin widened.

"Like the prince," he continued. "I wanted to wake you with a kiss. Unlike him, I expected to get a smack in the face." At the muffled oath from the ground floor his grin turned rueful.

"What's going on?"

"They're installing your refrigerator-freezer." Rafe spoke with a feigned nonchalance. Warily, he watched concern replace her confusion.

"I haven't ordered a refrigerator-freezer." Trudi pulled the covers up when she realized her t-shirt had slipped off her shoulder.

"Maybe not, but it's arrived." Rafe's quiet, firm tone stilled her attempts to swing her legs over the side of the bed. Once more their gazes met and clashed. "Get used to it, Trudi. I'm here. I'm staying. And I will provide for my daughter and her sister."

His daughter and her sister? Warmth seeped into her soul at his words and zeroed in on her heart. Rafe intended to accept Lizzie as his responsibility, Trudi realised with awe. At that moment she recognised the love she'd been too afraid to acknowledge previously.

She loved Rafe, and the revelation scared her witless!

In the bright afternoon sunlight, Trudi dared to hope. Perhaps he'd never come to love her, but he'd told her that the night of lovemaking they'd shared over a decade ago had been special for him. Was it enough to build a lifetime together?

The sound of muted hammer blows followed by a low rumble stunned Trudi back to the present. Alarmed, she forced her mind away from her dreams.

"What on earth is going on downstairs?"

"Washing machine." Rafe shrugged. "You needed a washing machine. It made sense to get everything installed at the same time. I'm afraid it means they'll spoil some of the work you've done, but I can help you repair and repaint."

"Repair?" she asked, not sure she wanted to hear the answer.

"They knocked out the pantry wall."

"Why?"

"It's the most convenient solution to the plumbing and creates enough space with the refrigerator-freezer to include a dining table. Later, we can add a utility room," Rafe offered.

"We?"

"Get used to it," Rafe repeated. "I may be sleeping and working at the Hall, but for the girls to get used to me as part of the family, I need to spend time with you. That means here."

He took her hand and pulled her off the bed and into his arms. "Don't be afraid," he said when she stiffened. "I need to hold you." He held her gently before scooping her robe from the end of the bed and draping it over her shoulders. "Go and get your shower. I'll be downstairs."

He ran a gentle finger down her cheek and left the room. In a daze, Trudi headed for the shower. The softness of the carpet beneath her bare feet penetrated her bewilderment. She looked down at the floor then let her gaze travel round the room. Where had the carpet and furniture come from? No doubt Rafe arranged it, but how and when? You couldn't furnish a whole room without creating some noise. How come she'd slept through it?

Trudi's eyes settled on the king size bed and the peach colored duvet cover. The large double wardrobe looked too heavy for one person to lift. Had Rafe brought it from the Hall?

No other solution fit the speed with which he'd furnished the whole room. This revealed a side to Rafe's character she'd only guessed at. She opened drawers and found her clothes neatly stashed in similar fashion to her room at the Hall. Hastily she selected fresh underwear, jeans, and a pink cotton shirt, and headed for the shower.

❦❦❦

The smell of freshly brewed coffee met her at the kitchen door, along with piles of brick rubble and dust.

"Goodness." Trudi peered at the builders' startled faces, and Rafe's wary expression, at the hand covering her mouth. "Thank you for giving us priority." She pasted a quick smile in place and took the mug of coffee Rafe offered her.

"You're welcome." The two men smiled at her before directing an evil grin in Rafe's direction.

What was that about? Trudi wondered and downed her drink.

"I suggest we eat at the Hall," Rafe remarked and headed for the front door.

Grabbing her jacket, Trudi followed him. "How did you manage to persuade them to do the job so quickly?"

"Incentives." He grinned over his shoulder. "Come on."

She placed her hand in his and let him lead her through the woods to the hall.

℘℘℘

"You should stay here for another night," Rafe said later that evening. The girls looked from Rafe to Trudi, waiting for her decision. Before she could speak, he turned to them. "The men are still working in the kitchen, and there's a lot of mess around. It will be easier if you to stay here for one more night." He watched their disappointment.

"Mum stayed at the farm last night," Rachel said. "Our stuff's there now" she added hopefully. "Please, Mum, you promised."

She'd slept there the night before?

How long had she slept? She'd assumed a couple of hours, but according to the girls, she stayed at the farm overnight. That meant she'd slept the clock round. No wonder the girls were peeved.

"I didn't know the men would be pulling walls down when I made that promise," Trudi explained to her daughter.

"It's not fair. You promised." Rachel tucked her chin into her chest and refused to meet her mother's eye.

"It's not safe for you to stay there tonight. You may have an accident if you forget about the work in the morning," Rafe said.

"Why should you care?" Rachel snapped, jumping up from her chair and glaring at him.

"Rachel, apologize at once for speaking to y—" Appalled at her near slip, Trudi stood up. "Now, Rachel. Apologise to Rafe for your bad manners."

Head bowed, Rachel apologized then ran from the room. Quietly, Lizzie slipped from her chair and followed Rachel.

"Damn it, Trudi," Rafe exploded. "When are you going to tell her the truth?"

"You don't understand."

"I understand you're prevaricating," he snapped. "And the longer you put it off the harder it will be and the bigger the shock to Rachel and Lizzie,"

His cell phone rang and Rafe picked it up. "Yes?" Without a backward glance, he left the room and Trudi to the company of her own thoughts. Slowly, she stood and went in search of the girls.

"Don't you like Rafe?" she asked Rachel when she found the girls in their old playroom.

Several boxes stuffed with toys stood just inside the doorway ready for Trudi to collect over the weekend. Lizzie sat on the wide windowsill with an old doll in her arms. Rachel sat on the floor with the contents of one box scattered in front of her.

"I do, but that doesn't give him the right to tell us what we can and can't do." Rachel dragged a book from the bottom of the box and laid it on her knee.

Crouched beside her daughter, Trudi wondered how to explain how much right Rafe had to show his concern for his daughter.

"Rachel, he cares for both you and Lizzie. Of course, he wouldn't want either of you to get hurt. When we left this afternoon, the men had taken down a wall in the kitchen and the rubble spread over the floor."

"Look! Uncle Vince has arrived," Lizzie interrupted.

Trudi stood up and crossed to stand at the window beside Lizzie and watched Vince's car come to a halt below their window. Cursing his lousy timing, Trudi left the room and ran down the stairs to meet him, the girls following close behind.

"What brings you here?" she asked.

"I remembered you said you wanted to move this weekend and came to offer my help." Vince smiled at Trudi before hugging the girls.

"We have a slight problem," Trudi offered.

"Rafe won't let us move in tonight," Rachel stated flatly.

"Why not?" Vince asked.

"Because he says it's not safe," Rachel huffed. "It's not fair. Mummy promised, and he won't let her keep it."

"I'm sure he has a good reason," Vince replied calmly before seeking Trudi's confirmation. "I thought he'd returned to Boston?" One eyebrow hiked up to his hairline.

"He did. Apparently, he arrived back here yesterday while I was at the farm."

"It was safe enough for Mum," Rachel interrupted.

"What's happened to make it unsafe since?" Intrigued, Vince arrowed a knowing glance at Trudi.

"He decided to order some kitchen equipment that necessitated the removal of the pantry wall." Over the girls' head she returned Vince's glance with a warning one of her own.

"He has no right to interfere," Rachel stormed.

☙❧

Rachel's sullen tone caught Rafe on the raw when he joined them.

"As your father, I have every right," he snapped.

A horrified silence filled the room. No one moved until a moan from Lizzie rocked Trudi out of her shock. She crossed to the stricken child.

"You're not my father. I hate you," Rachel screamed, pushing past him. She ran back upstairs to the playroom.

With a pleading request for Vince to look after his niece, Trudi followed her daughter.

"Can I come and live with you?" Lizzie beseeched her uncle.

Lizzie's frightened voice tore at Rafe's heart. He moved to crouch in front of her. "I hope you won't leave Rachel alone just now. You see I look on you as her sister." He wanted to hug the child but let his arms rest on his knees.

Vince's grip on his niece tightened, and he pulled her gently towards him.

"Not your brightest move, Hawk. If this is an example of your usual tactics with Trudi, I'm not surprised at your lack of success. I suggest you leave my niece to me." Vince's anger radiated clear 'no-go' parameters.

With a defeated sigh, Rafe rose, rubbed the back of his neck with his hand, and left the room.

What on earth possessed him to take his frustration out on his daughter, for God's sake? Would any of them ever forgive him for forcing the issue in such a crude and selfish manner?

He headed for his temporary office, opened the laptop and stared at the screen as the machine booted up, then paced from one side of the room to the other. He couldn't leave things as they stood, but where to start? He left the room, the luminosity from the laptop screensaver spilling an unearthly light across the walls. He had to find Trudi and apologize.

"I don't want to stay here anymore." Rachel's voice carried across the landing, Trudi's response too low to hear.

Muffled by the thick carpet, Rafe reached the open doorway without detection. Inside, Trudi sat crossed legged on the floor rocking back and forward, Rachel's arms clutching fiercely round her neck.

"It's a lie. Why did he lie?" The child's voice broke on a sob. "He wouldn't let us see you yesterday. He's trying to take you away from us." Her voice trembled with fear.

ᕷᕷᕷ

"He won't take me away from you," Trudi soothed.

More like the other way round. She felt like joining her daughter's crying binge. A movement in the doorway caught her eye and, spotting Rafe, she shook her head. Would he continue to ride roughshod over their lives, or would he respect her judgement and leave? After a tense hesitation, Rafe turned and disappeared from view. Rocking her daughter like a two-year-old, Trudi vowed she'd clarify their position with the arrogant man.

If he assumed coming back and dumping facts on the girls like that earned him the right to control their lives, he'd soon discover his mistake. One night's lust did not make him a father. The sadness in his eyes as he watched them together tugged at the edges of her anger, and she worked hard to keep it stoked and fuelled.

"Trudi?" She looked at Vince with Lizzie in his arms, standing in the doorway. "We have to talk."

"I know." She looked towards Lizzie, her head resting on her uncle's shoulder. "What did he hope to achieve?" Her voice flat, she patted the floor beside her and waited until Vince made himself comfortable and re-arranged Lizzie on his lap.

"Later. What are you going to do about the girls tonight?"

"I intended to stay here, but under the circumstances I've decided to take them to the farm. It may resemble a building site, but I don't want them waking up here in the morning."

Vince nodded agreement. "Best I speak to Rafe. Wait here and I'll take you over."

Carefully, Vince shifted the now sleeping Lizzie onto the floor allowing Trudi to wrap a comforting arm around the child.

⌇⌇⌇

"What the hell's the matter with you?" Vince swung away from his contemplation of the dark landscape beyond the window. "I mean, did you expect the girls to be delighted or something? When in reality, it sounded more like a threat." He raked his fingers through his hair and turned back to the dark window to watch Rafe's reflection.

"She's exhausted. When I arrived yesterday she could hardly stand." Guilt rolled through Rafe. "She won't let me help her."

Vince raised an eyebrow. "Why should she?" Pure sarcasm laced his words.

Rafe lifted his whiskey glass in front of his face. "As Rachel's father, I'm entitled to have some input into her safety."

Astonishment lit Vince's eyes. "No one can deny your paternity, nor are they. But butting right in and expecting Trudi to sit back and let you take the reins out of her hands after ten years of solo parenting is beyond arrogant. Give them a break, man. Of course, she's going to fight you when you suddenly start challenging her authority at every turn."

Exasperation warred with anger. "How could you be so cruel to Lizzie?" Vince struggled to control his emotions. "She's terrified you're going to take Rachel away from her. She's ten years old, for God's sake, and you—" He paused. "Out of the blue you dump your temper on her and Rachel." His hand sliced the air. "I'm warning you, Rafe, I'm on your case and watching you. My niece is Rachel's sister, and if you do anything to hurt either of those girls, you'll answer to me. Do I make myself clear?"

"Abundantly, Vince. But remember this, if I marry Trudi, Lizzie will become my daughter. Do you imagine for one moment I'd intentionally alienate either one of them?"

Shaking his head, Vince paced the floor and stopped in front of the other man. "Intentional or not, you did a damn fine job of it tonight. I'm taking them over to the farm, but I'll be back."

"No!" Rafe objected. "It's not safe. The girls may have an accident."

Eyes narrowed, Vince leaned towards Rafe. "Do you truly imagine I'll leave them exposed to such liabilities?" he demanded. "I'll make sure they can't walk straight into the mess. You can't assume the right to wrap them in cotton wool just because your parentage has been confirmed.

"To expect them to dance to your tune now you know about Rachel is pure lunacy and downright insulting to Trudi. And the rest of us, for that matter."

Vince straightened and made for the door, where he rested his hand on the knob. "A new father usually has nine months to become accustomed to the idea. Have a bit more faith in the mother of your child.

"If you let her, she'll help you build bridges with the girls. If you try and force her into a corner, you'll discover she'll come out fighting." With a lift of his shoulder, Vince left the room.

ഗ്രേ

The sound of the clock striking midnight welcomed them into the farmhouse. Trudi moved through the rooms turning on lights as she went, with Vince, carrying Lizzie, close behind her.

"Put her on my bed." Trudi leaned into her bedroom and snapped the light switch before moving aside to let Vince pass. "I'll move Lizzie's bed into Rachel's room so they can wake up together."

"Let me help you before I go back for Rachel. The shock's exhausted her. She'll sleep while we move the bed. Lead the way."

Vince followed Trudi across the landing, and together they soon rearranged the rooms.

Waiting for Vince to carry Rachel upstairs, Trudi gazed down at Lizzie. A frown creased the child's brow. Even in sleep, the evening's events seemed to be plaguing her. Trudi's heart broke for her. At a time when she'd lost her only parent, her friend and sister acquired a father who now threatened Lizzie's world as she knew it. Trudi brushed a gentle finger across Lizzie's cheek and discovered tears.

"I've put Rachel on her bed. While you get her more comfortable, I'll bring Lizzie through." Vince moved round the bed and reached to pick her up.

"She's crying in her sleep." Trudi whispered, ducking her head before heading to the girls' room. The tears stung the back of her lids. She wished could give in to her emotions and howl at the moon.

ొఁఒ

"Leave that." Vince took the dustpan and brush from Trudi's fingers. "If I move the sofa across the access to the kitchen, the girls will have to climb over it. That'll remind them to stay out of the way. Come." He led Trudi to a comfy chair and gently pushed her down. "It's late, or should I say early?" A quick glance at his watch revealed two hours passed since their arrival.

"I wanted to be sure they wouldn't fall over the rubble." Trudi didn't voice her fear that if the girls hurt themselves, Rafe might try to move them back to the Hall. "What did he say?"

Vince followed her abrupt change of subject. "He's aware of the damage he's done," he said slowly. "He's frightened you'll try to keep him away from Rachel."

"I want to. Believe me, Vince. Oh, how I want to. But what good will it do? It won't settle anything. I just wish he'd kept his mouth shut." Trudi sighed. "I'll have to talk to him, but not until I've spoken to the girls."

"He understands they come first. I had a go at him for unsettling Lizzie as well as upsetting Rachel. I'm afraid I lost my temper."

Trudi sighed again. "Understandable, under the circumstances." Frowning, she leaned forward and stared at her feet, her clasped hands hanging between her knees. "I'd hoped the growing attachment between the three of them during the summer would have carried us through. But I'm afraid the girls may never forgive him now. I don't know what to do."

The tears she'd tried to hold back slipped down her face unheeded. She grieved for her frightened girls and for her own shattered dreams.

※※※

Rafe stared at the haggard complexion reflecting back at him. "You stupid son-of-a-bitch!"

The pale light of dawn filtering through his bedroom window cast deep shadows on one side of his face. His reflection remained silent.

"You let your temper overrule your common sense and compassion." His hand crashed onto the surface of the table. The mirror shook in response. "What the hell can I do now that won't exacerbate the situation?"

His cell phone rang. The sound startled him into dropping it when he reached to snatch it off the bed stand. From beneath the bed where it fell, the phone continued its shrill demand for attention.

"Yes?" he snapped.

"Is this a bad time to call?" His mother's gentle voice filled his ear.

Taking a deep breath, Rafe tried to pull himself together. "I blew it."

"What did you blow?" His mother's concern travelled across the ether.

Rafe struggled to explain the events of the previous night. "Rachel declared she hates me and never wants to see me again. And Vince—" Memories of the night before closed his throat.

"What about him, dear?" she prompted. "Vince?"

"When I told the girls I was Rachel's father—" A gasp from the other end interrupted him. He waited for his mother's response, and when she remained silent, he continued. "When I told them," he repeated. "Lizzie ran to her uncle and asked if she could go and live with him."

"And Trudi? What was her reaction?"

"Vince took them back to the farm."

"That's understandable."

"You don't understand, Mom." His words tumbled over themselves. "I ordered some structural alterations to the kitchen, and the builders left brick rubble all over the place. The girls may have an accident."

"Let me get this straight." Even as an adult, that precise tone of his mother's voice never failed to reduce him to the realms of a recalcitrant ten-year-old. "Are you saying you interfered with Trudi's home?"

"Only for the best," Rafe explained. "She needed a fridge."

"Rafe, whatever your opinion, it doesn't entitle you to rampage through her life or that of those girls."

"But I'm Rachel's father," he protested.

"God, give me strength." His mother's muttered oath travelled across the Atlantic unheeded. "Rafe, do you remember how you felt when you discovered Daniel paid for your schooling?" The stunned silence that followed revealed more than words. "I think you're beginning to understand."

His mother's sharp tone cleared his mind.

"I'll call you back later," Rafe replied. "Thanks Mom."

He clicked his phone shut and stuffed it in his back pocket. With a wink at the now cheerful reflection in his mirror, Rafe left his room and took the stairs two at a time.

The rich aroma of coffee greeted him when he entered the kitchen and found Judy whipping eggs in a bowl and waiting for the toaster to divest itself of its contents.

"Scrambled eggs?" She waved a pan in his direction.

Rafe helped himself to coffee. "Sounds wonderful."

ごごご

Irritated by the sound of Rafe's buoyant tone, Vince wrapped his arms around Judy when he entered the kitchen, and gave her a smacking kiss on the cheek before turning towards Rafe.

"You're surprisingly cheerful this morning."

"Thanks to my remarkable mother. In a few words she reminded me of how I reacted when I discovered Daniel Kinsale paid for my architectural studies."

Judy plunked plates heaped with fresh toast and soft fluffy scrambled eggs in front of both men. "Eat that before it gets cold," she ordered before joining them at the table. "Are either of you going over to the farm this morning?" she asked.

Vince nodded. Rafe shook his head.

"Perhaps you'll take that casserole and trifle over with you. With the disruption in her kitchen, it'll be easier for her to simply put a casserole in the oven. And trifle is the girls' favorite."

☙❧☙

Rafe squirmed as Judy's words hitched a ride on his growing guilt. He pushed his empty plate into the center of the table and reached for his mug. It was empty, too. Pushing his chair back, he refilled his mug and held the container towards the others still seated at the table. Judy shook her head. Vince nodded.

Rafe filled Vince's mug then hesitated. "Before you leave for the farm, can we have a word?"

Vince studied Rafe's features. "Very well."

Judy shot a startled glance in Vince's direction and shifted her chair back from the table.

"I'll load these plates in the dishwasher and leave you two alone," she informed them brightly.

The two men watched her moving around the room. They remained silent until her footsteps faded down the hallway.

"Well?" Vince kicked back in his chair and waited.

"I can apologize for last night, but it doesn't change anything." Rafe leaned forward, resting his elbows on the table. "This morning, my mother reminded me of my reaction when my birth father interfered in my life. I'll do whatever Trudi and the girls want."

"Which means what?" Vince never moved, his eyes narrowed, focussed on Rafe.

"It means," he said, shifting in his chair, "I still intend to be there for them, but not on my terms. Not yet anyway."

"It's not a matter of whose terms, Rafe," Vince said slowly. "It's a matter of compromise. Give Trudi time, and she'll come round. But you have to be prepared to give, too. Last night's 'bull-in-a-china-shop' attitude demonstrates what happens when one person tries to control another."

"I'm not walking away. I love Trudi and both girls. I'm telling you now—I'll do whatever it takes to win them round."

CHAPTER 15

"Why should he care about me?" Lizzie's tearful query hung in the still air. "I'm not his daughter."

"No." Rachel's hesitation reached both listeners. Lizzie's tears increased and Rafe's guilt hitched up another notch. "But you're my sister and Mummy's daughter. He can't change that."

Rafe smiled when her belligerent tone reached him where he stood at the edge of the wood. His daughter's logic was indisputable.

"Maybe not," Lizzie muttered. "But it won't make him love me."

Rafe's smile disappeared. Before he changed his mind, he moved towards the children.

"Lizzie? Rachel? Are you there? Can I ask your advice about something?" He paused a few yards away and waited for their response. Never again would he force them to take sides.

Rachel's glare almost destroyed his resolution. "What do you want?"

"I'd like to talk with you, if I may?"

Rachel glanced at Lizzie who moved closer to her and nodded. She said something Rafe couldn't hear.

Still glaring at him, Rachel patted the ground.

Careful not to get too close, Rafe hunkered down in front of them. "First." He worked through the words he wanted to say in his head before continuing. "I'm sorry for upsetting you last week. It was wrong of me."

Everything he'd rehearsed during the week since his disastrous revelation scrambled in his mind. The girls remained silent and watchful.

"Your mother asked me to wait. I didn't listen to her. And in not listening, I hurt both of you. All of you," he amended. "And I made it worse. I wanted to help you both. And your mother. But I went about it the wrong way and caused more distress." His hand fluttered through the air in front of him. "Sometimes—"

He stopped and started again. "Sometimes we do things with the best intentions, but they don't work. That's what happened last week when I interfered with your Mom's kitchen. I wanted to help and I made it worse instead."

"But you told us to stay at the Hall when you let Mum stay at the Farm. It wasn't fair. Mum promised, and you wanted her to break it."

Rafe sensed the unspoken words lining up behind her defiant gaze. His daughter had spirit, and manners, and right now her manners were winning over her wish to tell him where to go. Careful to hide his smile, he nodded.

"Unintentionally, yes, I did," he admitted. "It was one more mistake I made. If possible, I'd change what happened last week, but I can't. I hope you'll both give me another chance." He waited for a response.

The unspoken link between the children astounded him. It took one long glance for them to decide.

"Why are you here?" For the first time Lizzie directed her question to him.

Another minefield opened in front of him. Rafe hoped to speak with Trudi before approaching the girls, now Lizzie's question blew another good intention skywards.

"I've come to ask your Mom if I may introduce you to some people who are very special to me."

"Who?" Rachel challenged.

"My parents." Unaware of holding his breath, he watched a myriad of emotions flit across his daughter's face.

"Would they be my grandparents?" she asked after a pause.

"Yes." Again Rafe waited.

"They're not my grandparents, though."

"Is Rachel your sister?" Rafe held Lizzie's dejected gaze.

She nodded.

"Then my parents are your grandparents, too. How could they be anything else?" His question hung in the air.

"But you're Rachel's daddy, not mine." Her voice hitched as she tried to swallow her tears.

Rafe opened his arms, and with a smile at his daughter, wrapped his arms around her sister when she climbed into his lap. "You would make me very happy if you'd let me be your dad, Lizzie."

"What about Mummy?" Rachel's question tugged at his heart.

"I love your Mom, Rachel—"

"Why aren't you married to her?" Anger sparked from the silver-gray eyes staring at him. How had he'd missed their similarity to his own before now? And how did he answer the question?

"I swear if I'd known of your existence, I would have married your mom."

"How come you didn't know?"

How could he expect a child to understand the circumstances of that stormy night, when adults had problems believing what happened?

"We lost touch before your mum knew about you." He wished he knew how much Trudi had revealed to them before he said anything else. "Hasn't your mom mentioned it to you?"

Rachel shook her head, and Rafe caught the glint of tears in her eyes.

"Perhaps we should talk more about this when we're together," he suggested.

Rachel studied his face before nodding. Rafe held out his hand, and Rachel placed her small one in his. He looked down at the child in his lap to find her watching him intently. He bent his head forward and brushed a light kiss on her forehead.

"I love you both."

His simple words held a wealth of promise. The girls smiled back at him.

ഇഇഇ

An idle glance out the bedroom window stopped Trudi in her tracks. Her duster slipped unheeded from her fingers, and fear engulfed her. Even from this distance she sensed the children's misgivings as they listened to something Rafe said. Her cleaning forgotten, she stayed at the window—not caring if she was discovered—until the three of them stood and headed for the house.

Perhaps one day she'd tolerate the constant company of fear and apprehension that thoughts of Rachel and Rafe together invoked. She headed for the kitchen and reached it at the same time Rachel and Lizzie barrelled through the back door. Rafe, she noticed, didn't automatically follow them inside.

"May I come in?"

One eyebrow raised in amazement, she nodded and stepped back to let him to enter the refurbished kitchen and glance towards the newly installed refrigerator-freezer and washing machine. "Thank you." With a wave, Trudi pointed to the new equipment.

"I'm sorry." Rafe hesitated, moved forward and lifted one of her hands. "I meant well, but I realize I went about it the wrong way. I'll try not to repeat the mistake."

She noticed his wry grin deepened the laughter lines around his eyes.

"I know. I've had time to think during the past week. I've always relied on my own judgement, and it's going to take time for me to adjust." When she looked up, Trudi discovered a warm smile had replaced the wry grin.

"Together we'll get there, I promise you."

The soft brush of his fingertips along the back of her hand sent goose bumps up her arm and a warmth to her cheeks. Gently, she withdrew her hand and headed for the kettle.

Holding it up, she asked, "Tea? Coffee?"

"Neither, thanks. I've come to ask a favor."

With great care, Trudi replaced the kettle in its holder. "Ask."

"My parents are visiting with me and would like to meet their grandchildren. I've come to ask all of you over to the Hall."

At the back of her mind, Trudi registered the girls' anticipation. "Now?" She ran her hands over her work-dusty jeans then realized Rafe's eyes had followed their course down her hips. "I'm not dressed for company."

"I'd say you're fine as you are, but I understand if you'd rather change. I'm happy to wait."

"If your parents want to meet the children, you don't need me." She wasn't ready for any of this, she realized. Afraid her legs would give way beneath her, she gripped the cabinet behind her for support. "Girls go and clean up and change."

She noticed their relieved smiles before they made for the stairs. Whatever passed between them in the garden, it seemed they'd resolved their differences with Rafe.

"I won't try to force you, but I would like you to join us." The warmth of his voice trickled along her skin.

"Why? Your parents want to meet the children."

Rafe walked to the window and gazed out at the rapidly transforming garden. "On my way here, I overheard Lizzie and Rachel talking. Lizzie's worried I won't love her because she's not my natural daughter. I spent a few moments with them before coming to see you, but there's something I want Lizzie to hear. And it will be better if you're present."

"What?"

"It will be easier if you join us." He retraced his steps and stopped in front of her, his anxious gaze holding hers.

Trudi waited, uncertain, half expecting Rafe to pressure her, surprised when he didn't.

"I won't be long. Make yourself a drink or something if you want." She tried to smile, failed, spun on her heels, and fled upstairs.

ᏭᎧᏭᎧ

His arms ached with the need to hold her. His heart ached for the grief he'd caused her. And his body pulsed with desire for her. Rafe hoped the conversation he was about to force on his unsuspecting parents wouldn't destroy everything he held dear.

He looked around the kitchen, noticing the freshly decorated walls and new tiles on the floor, and sniffed the air. A fresh batch of bread cooling on a rack caught his attention. The ping of the oven timer made him jump. Had Trudi heard it?

He glanced towards the stairs. No approaching footsteps reached him, so he bent down and looked into the oven. Before he found an oven-mitt or tea towel, Trudi's light tread alerted him to her nearness.

"Your timer's gone off."

He straightened and watched her grab a mitt off the counter-top. He inhaled the rich warm smell of sponge cake as she placed the little cakes on another cooling rack.

A sound from the door drew Rafe's gaze away from Trudi's flushed face. Rachel and Lizzie stood together, clasping hands. Their clothing caught his attention. They wore identical denim shirts and jeans. Their socks matched, as did their trainers. Identical clasps held their hair away from their faces, and the same anxious look zeroed in on their mother. He sucked in a breath, his astonishment at their similarity, rendering him silent.

When Trudi opened her arms wide they both rushed into her waiting embrace, and wrapped their arms around Trudi's neck.

"It'll be okay." Her quiet encouragement revealed her intent to show a united front.

The bond between the two girls matched, even exceeded, the closest twins Rafe had ever known. His admiration and pride in them grew. Would his parents recognise their strategy? His mother would, he decided with a grin.

Half an hour later his assumption proved correct. His mother's startled gaze flew from the children to meet his eyes.

"What beautiful girls." Martha turned to Trudi. Rafe heaved a silent sigh of relief when his mother avoided mentioning their previous meeting. "I'm so pleased you've come. Have you settled in at the farm?"

While his mother gently encouraged Trudi to talk about her move and how much the girls enjoyed their new home, Rafe joined his step-father, drawing the girls with him. Pleasure engulfed him when they both slid their hands into his as they studied Jess's Native American features.

"You don't look much like your dad."

Lizzie's comment drew his mother's gaze towards them. Desperately, he tried to communicate his silent plea with his eyes. Everything rested on the next few minutes.

"No we're not alike, Lizzie." Aware of the silence filling the room, he held his father's alert stare. Rafe stepped in front of Lizzie and bent his knees until their faces were level. "Do you mind if I tell my dad what we were talking about earlier?"

"Rafe?" The alarm in Trudi's voice was mirrored in Rafe's parent's faces. "What's going on?"

"You have little reason to, but please trust me on this, Trudi." Rafe watched her move beside him. He turned his pleading eyes towards his mother.

"Lizzie?" Trudi took hold of her child's hand. Rachel moved to the other side of her sister.

"Rafe?" He saw fear in his mother's eyes. "Do you know what you're doing?"

He crossed the room and wrapped his hand round her trembling fingers. "I love Trudi, and when she's ready I hope she'll marry me." He heard Trudi's gasp and the girls' swift movement but never dropped his gaze from his mother's eyes. "It will all come out. It's important we talk about it now."

"What about Megan and Luke, about their reactions when they find out?"

"Believe me, I've thought of little else since I discovered how vital Trudi is to my existence." He sat on the arm of his mother's chair and put his arm around her shoulder.

"Today when I went to ask Trudi and the girls to visit with us, I overheard something Lizzie said. And she needs to understand if Trudi and Vince agree, I want to adopt her as my daughter, too. I already love her as if she were mine."

His mother turned toward her husband, and Rafe felt rather than saw their unspoken agreement.

"Thank you."

Rafe brushed a kiss across his mother's cheek and squeezed her hand, before returning to take hold of one of Lizzie's. Across her head, he met and held Trudi's eyes with his own. *Later.*

He telegraphed the silent message to her and watched her lips curve in a tremulous smile. He turned his attention back to Lizzie and hunkered down beside her.

"My dad is proof a man can love all his children the same, even if one of them isn't his."

"How many children do you have?" Lizzie turned to face his dad.

"Three."

Rafe watched her silently weighing up his father's response. Had she worked it out yet? He looked across at Trudi's dawning recognition before she turned toward his mother, who nodded, and then back to Jess, the man he'd always known as Dad.

"I was present at Rafe's birth, but genetically he isn't mine. In every other way, Rafe is my son." Jess spoke directly to Lizzie. "I loved him before his birth, and I'll love him until the day I die, the same way I love my daughter Megan and my other son Luke."

Two pairs of round eyes stared up at him.

"That's right," Rafe told the children. "My dad loves me the same way he loves my sister and brother. And I want you to know I can love you, Lizzie, as much as if you were a child of my flesh. I do love you and will always love you, whatever happens between your Mom and me.

⌘⌘⌘

Stunned by Rafe's public declaration of love, Trudi hardly took in the conversation between Lizzie, Rafe, and his father. As the words settled in her mind, she looked across to his mother and saw tears streaming down her face. Swiftly, she crossed the room and sat on the arm Rafe so recently vacated.

"Kinsale?"

Rafe's mother nodded.

"I gather your daughter and other son don't know?" Again Mrs. Hawk nodded. Putting her arm around the older woman, Trudi rested her head against Martha's. "I understand."

Martha stiffened and tried to pull away, but Trudi continued speaking in a low tone. "Several hours are still missing of the night I met your son. And may I never recall them. After your daughter's visit, I lived with the fear Rafe would snatch Rachel and keep her in America. I believed you'd gang up against me and sue for custody."

"My son would never have done that to you."

"Hindsight is a wonderful thing, but please understand, my only experience of marriage was less than stellar. And the events I do remember didn't show the better side of your son. I spent most of the following months hiding from my husband and may never remember what happened immediately after we escaped from his house.

"I thought Rafe only wanted to marry me to get close to his daughter. My fear meant Rachel discovered her parentage in a manner no child should have to experience. Please don't let that happen to your children."

Giving Martha a brief hug, Trudi moved to sit closer to her daughters. They both sat on Jess's knee, listening to him relate many of Rafe's childhood adventures. She watched Rafe join his mother and talk quietly to her.

She needed time to think and headed for the main kitchen to gather a tea tray, coffee, and biscuits.

Could they make a future together? He'd told his parents he loved her. And in his determination to prove to Lizzie he would love her as much as Rachel, he did it in a way to prevent another rift between them. He'd risked everything for a little girl who loved his daughter like the sister she'd become.

Her heart swelled with pride knowing Rafe loved her too. The man had told her she'd given him a night of love he'd never forgotten.

Since his arrival, he'd stimulated emotions she'd never experienced before, taken her to heights and depths she'd never imagined. Never again would she live in the frozen limbo ruling her before he re-entered her life.

The discovery, like a key, unlocked the last chains of fear from around her heart. She experienced a physical lifting of her spirits. In that moment, she understood the saying "lifting a weight off your shoulders." She felt taller, straighter, and full of happy, fizzing bubbles of joy.

The fear of discovery no longer held her hostage to her emotions. She loved Rafe so much. And now she could share her love openly with him, unafraid of rejection.

The clack of the kettle switching off drew her attention back to her surroundings. She collected mugs, milk, sugar, and the filled teapot and set them on the tray.

"Hey, let me carry that."

Surprised by Rafe's quiet approach, Trudi nearly dropped the laden tray.

"Oh my! You startled me." Her voice trailed away when he lifted the tray from her nerveless fingers and set it back on the table.

"This is hardly the setting I imagined, but I love you so much, Trudi. Will you marry me?"

He held up his hand to prevent her responding. "No. Don't say anything now. I don't want to rush you into anything you're not ready for."

"But—"

"Trudi, I love you more than life itself. I want to share the rest of my days with you and have more babies with you. But I understand your fears, and I'll try to be patient. Together we can work through them." He reached for her hand and cradled it to his cheek.

"I'm sorry I didn't tell you how much I love you to your face, but I was afraid you wouldn't believe me." He turned her hand over in his and kissed her palm.

"When I overheard Lizzie tell Rachel it wouldn't be possible for me to love her, I had to bring her back to meet my dad. I had to prove to her I can and do love her, the same way I love Rachel. I told them I love you, and Rachel asked why we'd never married. I told her truthfully, we'd lost touch, and I didn't know about her." He brushed his lips over her fingers and nibbled her thumb.

"If you ever want to tell her about the missing hours, I'll be beside you, sweetheart. Remember, I love you. Always."

Rafe let his lips pay homage to each finger-tip in turn then cupped her face with both hands.

Stunned at the emotion pouring from him, Trudi let him take her face between his hands and place a swift, hard kiss on her lips before he picked up the tray and started out of the kitchen.

The idea of wasting another moment galvanised her into action.

"Rafe?" She watched him turn towards her, love darkening his smoky gray eyes to polished silver.

"Yes?"

"I love you, too."

The tray clattered to the floor unheeded. Rafe leaped over the mess, pulled her into his arms, and showered her with kisses.

"Is that a yes?"

"Yes," Trudi gasped with a laugh when Rafe lifted his mouth long enough for her to respond. "Yes. Yes. Yes, I love you. And yes, I'll marry you."

Neither saw their daughters and Rafe's parents standing in the doorway, their concern replaced with jubilant smiles at the sight of Trudi enveloped in Rafe's arms.

THE END

ABOUT THE AUTHOR

Sherry Gloag is a transplanted Scot now living in the beautiful coastal countryside of Norfork, England. She considers the surrounding countryside an extension of her own garden, to which she escapes when she needs "thinking time" and solitude to work out the plots for her next novel. While out walking, she enjoys talking to her characters—as long as there are no other walkers close by.

Apart from writing, Gloag enjoys gardening, walking, and reading. She cheerfully admits her books tend to take over most of the shelf and floor space in her workroom-cum-office. She also finds crystal craft work therapeutic.

Visit Sherry at: http://www.sherrygloag.com

ALSO FROM BLACK OPAL BOOKS

MY KILLER, MY LOVE
by Mona Karel

CLUBBED TO DEATH
JORDAN DAVIS MYSTERIES – BOOK 2
by Alyssa Lyons

BLOOD FEST: CHASING DESTINY
by Pepper O'Neal

LAST WISHES
JORDAN DAVIS MYSTERIES – BOOK 1
by Alyssa Lyons

DUTY CALLS
by Sherry Gloag

CRAIGS' LEGACY
by Terry Campbell